Cattle Prod

J. ANDREW THOMAS

Also by J. Andrew Thomas

Available at jandrewthomas.com

Suburban Purgatory Hell

Mauled by Death in the Hot Rain

Staring into the Void of Destruction

College is for Losers

The Garden Gnomes are Watching

*Sometimes You Get Lucky and the Problem Fixes
Itself*

Poems for Another Day

To Dr. T.
who pushed me a little
farther

Cattle Prod

November 7, 1996

Two years was enough. I sat on the bench and didn't play for two long god damn years. I never missed a practice, I did everything I was told, was by far the fastest player on the team and still never saw more than a few minutes of playing time in a game, and that's if I was lucky. It wasn't even that I was a bad soccer player; I just wasn't one of *them*. The coach knew right away who was going to play from the start, it was a rigged system. It was like I was a band groupie or a reporter following the team around instead of an actual player.

My parents showed up for a few games hoping to see me play but after a while I told them it was pointless. Waving to them from the bench every game was humiliating. When I walked to my dad's car after the last game was over, I felt a wave of freedom wash over me like never before. There were no more practices after school every day and then games on the weekend; I could do whatever I wanted now! I still had to go to school though. That was a big problem.

I'm only a sophomore and I want out bad. It feels more like prison, I'm forced to go to school against my will. It's not fair. But at least soccer is over forever; I have to focus on the little victories to keep me going.

I'm going to start keeping a journal again. I'm at a point where I feel more lost than ever. It'll be easy now that I have all this free time. I don't have anybody to talk to about my problems and typing them out *does* make me feel better. Maybe I'll look back on this stuff when I'm a happy adult and laugh at how "miserable" my life was. I hope so.

November 8, 1996

I sat down in 5th period study hall today and as usual Darcy was talking to her upperclassman boyfriend, Matt Reinhart, right outside the doorway. They did this every day. They acted like the 50 minutes of class that they wouldn't see each other would be an eternity. It made me sick that they could be so happy. The bell rang, and she came strolling in with a big smile on her face as she sat next to me.

I have been in love with Darcy Kirkman since I saw her stroll into history class on the first day of school last year. Her long brown hair, plump ass, and those perfect field hockey legs in that green Catholic school girls skirt did me in good. She is definitely very pretty but isn't the cliché Barbie doll "hot" by any standard. I think that is why I'm attracted to her. Conventional beauty always bored me. She is half beauty, half bad-ass which is so much better than the girls who are bleach blonde, caked in makeup, and have nothing to say.

I lusted after her for all of freshman year and never said a word to her. It killed me. I met her by chance when she sat at the end of our lunch table this year. My group of outcasts I'm friends with: Ralph, Bill, and Greg, are at one end of the table, and Darcy and her chunky friend Cecilia are at the other. It took a few weeks, but we wore them down enough until they started to talk to us. Once that happened, they couldn't get enough of how goofy we acted. When you're a nobody, you have to use self-deprecating comedy to make fun of yourself to disarm the other people.

I should just be happy that she talks to me.

Actually, thinking about it, it makes it worse that I have to hear about her dating a string of assholes. They just use her, and I think she uses them. I don't know; I've never dated a girl, so I have no clue how they think or why they do the things they do.

When she sat down today in Study Hall, I told her that I quit soccer for good. She sighed and said I should do something else with my time because colleges are going to want to see activities or sports. I told her I didn't care about college or really anything for that matter.

"Hey Nic, why don't you kick for the football team?" she said sarcastically.

I laughed it off as the most ridiculous thing I had ever heard. Then the bell rang and Mr. Donner let out a big bellow about shutting the hell up and everyone got quiet.

Most teachers wouldn't have been able to talk like this but not Mr. Donner, he didn't give a crap. He was a big hulk of a man with a deep voice. We nicknamed him Fred Gwynn because he looked like Herman Munster from *The Munster's* TV show. I'm always quiet, so it doesn't matter to me. The people who talk get an immediate boot and are sent to the disciplinarian's office, Mr. Girard, who is a real hard ass.

I never did much in study hall; usually I doodled in my copy book. I couldn't even draw so I just drew shapes and shaded them in. As I doodled, I started to think about what Darcy said.

Was she just making a joke and messing with me, or was she serious? It had to be a joke. A skinny loser like me who couldn't even get on the soccer field wouldn't have a shot with those football gods. Still, the thought stayed with me the rest of the day, and the more I thought about it, the more the fantasy seemed like a possibility.

As I sat there in study hall, bored as hell, I envisioned myself lining up for a game winning kick in front of a stadium full of kids who previously didn't know I existed. The ball is snapped and I boot the winning field goal. The team carries me off and I'm a hero.

I snapped back into reality and looked around the study hall. God do I have a ridiculous imagination, I thought. It's really the only thing that gets me through these long school days.

November 10, 1996

Now that soccer is over, I have time to get back to my real passion: movies. I used to love television so much as a kid. I would watch it every day for hours and hours. I was shy and didn't socialize that much, so television was a way for me to watch people interact and not have to participate. It made me feel like I wasn't alone when I had nobody to play with.

I would watch anything from Gilligan's Island to Andy Griffith to Alf. It was mostly rerun's on cable that came out before my time, but I loved it all. I didn't get into movies until last year. My obsession started when Bill from lunch told me to watch the movie *Clerks*. I had never heard of it and thought it was going to be really stupid because he said it was in black and white. "It's really funny though," he kept saying. So, I took his advice and rented it one lonely Friday night.

I have a nice VCR and a small 13 inch TV in my room. I had saved up money from my job at McDonald's for three months and treated myself. It was over 250 dollars for the setup but it was the greatest decision I ever made.

Most people like to watch movies on a big TV with other people on a couch with popcorn. Not me. I don't mind and actually prefer to watch TV alone. I wonder if there's something wrong with me. Everyone else seems to love being around as many people as possible. I don't know why, but I get so anxious about what to say or how I look when I'm around a group of people. Just being popular and having a ton of friends, I wonder how they decide who to hang out with.

My preference for isolation probably stemmed from being locked in my house summer after summer while both of my parents were at work. I could do whatever I wanted as long as the grass was cut and the chores were complete. When they were done, I would just sit alone and watch. It was amazing. I loved laughing and laughing; it took me away from the world. My motto was, if I'm laughing, how can I be sad? My mom even said that to me one time.

"The only time I see you smiling is when you are watching TV."

She was right.

Anyway, I popped *Clerks* in my VCR that night, and it was like nothing I had ever seen. It was this low budget "independent" movie that was fucking hilarious. They were all nobodies in the movie - no movie stars whatsoever. I had only seen big budget stuff before that. This cheap independent film was so much better than all of them! From then on, I wanted to find more and more obscure movies that I hadn't seen.

The latest one I rented was *The Basketball Diaries*. It was this crazy movie about some high school kid who was a basketball player and a heroin addict. It said on the box it was based on a true story, but I don't know, it seemed a little farfetched. How could this kid be on heroin and be a great basketball player? What high school kid is doing heroin? I've never seen anything but weed.

Since I watch so many movies I think I am going to start rating them from 1-5 stars. Then I'll have a record of what I watched, and which ones were good.

Clerks: 5/5 stars

The Basketball Diaries: 3/5 stars

November 13, 1996

I had Mr. Donner for Theology as well. He liked to show us videos from time to time. Today, he showed us one called *Life is Worth Living*. It was some Catholic propaganda video that interviewed people who were suicidal and were testifying that praying and going to church changed their lives, and they didn't want to die anymore. I looked around in the darkness during the video and no one was paying attention. What a crock, I thought. Praying and going to church wouldn't make me feel better. I'll have to do it myself.

When I was down during those first two years of high school soccer, I prayed to God every day to have a better life. He didn't listen. The church just likes to brainwash impressionable kids and down and out adults. What bullshit. It's time to do something on my own. Nobody is going to do anything for me, not even the almighty "God."

November 15, 1996

Even though I was done with soccer, I still had to put up with the captain of the soccer team, Marshall Gomer, at McDonald's. He was the epitome of "rich white kid." He had one of those snarky faces that made you want to punch him.

When I applied to McDonald's freshman year, Marshall was already working there. I didn't know this. I got the job, and the first day I was being trained, he showed up like he owned the place. All the girls loved him. He looked at me and said "Really? You're working at *my* McDonald's?" I guess he thought I wasn't cool enough to work there. I just looked at him and said "Yea man." It was the first time he talked to me. He never said anything to me on the soccer field.

McDonald's is actually a decent place to work. Most of the kids are in high school and there are a ton of hot chicks who work there. I'm too shy to talk to them though. I only say something if they talk to me. I like working the drive through because I can sit back there behind the old Ronald McDonald statue that they don't use anymore and nobody bothers me. When we get slow, I usually day dream about funny TV shows that I watched. It gets me through the day.

The upfront cashier is the worst. You get to see more people and it's busier, which makes the day go faster, but they make you clean when there are no customers. Also, Marshall's friends from Lindsburg Catholic will come in and try to get free food. I didn't know this the first time they came in and charged them full price. Word got back to Marshall, and he got so pissed at me saying "If you see my friends, always give them free shit!"

It makes me nervous because there is a camera pointed right at the cash register. It's easy to ring them up for one burger and give them five but I've never been the criminal type. I'm filled with anxiety whenever I have to steal. I didn't understand the rush some kids get from shoplifting.

I'm happy I don't have to work today. I just went in, picked up my check, and then went home. I have to work tomorrow though…for eight long hours. It's brutal. Saturdays used to be so fun when I was a kid and now I just work in a drive thru, serving junk food to obese people for $5.25 an hour. Hopefully Marshall isn't there tomorrow. That's all I hope for.

November 22, 1996

Well, it's been an eventful week. I finally tried kicking a football. It was harder than it looked! I didn't even know anything about it either. I was too embarrassed to ask someone how to kick a football. I was worried they would laugh at the mere concept of me trying to kick a field goal. Luckily my Dad watched the Philadelphia Eagles every week so I sat down with him on Sunday to watch what the kickers did. I pretended to be interested in the football game instead of telling him what I was doing. It was kind of shocking to him at first.

"What are you doing here? Shouldn't you be playing video games or something?" he said sipping his can of cheap beer.

"I just wanted to check out the game. I might start watching," I said.

"Oh. Well, if you have any questions, let me know."

I didn't know much about football. I knew the quarterback, running back, and wide receivers. That was about it. I liked playing sports, but watching them bored the hell out of me. There were so many good movies and TV shows with interesting stories and characters I could be watching instead. A bunch of guys beating the hell out of each other didn't interest me.

We sat there and both cheered. He even let me have a beer. It ended up being kind of fun. I was secretly focused on the kickers though. I studied their every move. It was hard though, TV didn't like to show them that much. They never got a replay. It took the whole game but I got that they took three steps back and two steps over to kick a field goal. They didn't even run up to it, it was just a slow glide and it was all leg strength. The kick offs were harder to tell. They were much farther back so it was hard to tell how many steps it was. I think it is 10 or 11 steps back and four to the left. They made it look so easy; I was ready to try it myself.

Later that day I went out to the shed and found an old football. It was deflated so I pumped it up with the air compressor and made a makeshift tee out of a piece of wood. I just angled it on the top of the ball. It looked stupid but it worked. Then, I put on my soccer cleats and went out to the back yard and set the ball up in front of the shed. I took three steps back and two steps left just like the pros did it. I ran up towards the ball and swung my foot with full force. All I saw was dirt flying everywhere. The ball dribbled towards the shed, and my foot took a severe beating. I hopped around the yard in pain. It was horrible! I almost gave up right there.

20 minutes later, when my foot started to feel better, I set it up again. This time, I did a slow walk and softly hit the ball. Surprisingly it hit the shed with some power and it bounced back and almost hit me.

From there, I kicked into the shed for about an hour, hitting about half of the balls cleanly. The other half were line drives that wouldn't have a chance of going through the uprights. The crazy thing was that I had more fun doing that by myself than playing on the soccer team.

I woke up the next day with a sore foot. I could barely walk on it. Even though I hurt, I wasn't down. I knew that this was the start of something good. When I tried to lift weights for the first time, I was sore as hell the next day, but then in a week I was used to it. This was the same thing. Now that I have free time after school, there is an unlimited amount of time to practice and nobody will know what I am doing. I am so afraid of what people would think. This will be my secret.

November 23, 1996

I just got back from a normal Saturday night. Let me take you through what "our kind" does instead of dating and parties and dances.

1) I tell my parents I want to hang out with Ralph, so they drop me off at his house.

I met Ralph in 8th grade when the teacher was assigning desks by name. We were the last two at the end of the alphabet so she put our desks together. Ever since then we've been friends. He likes fishing, cars and Nintendo, so it worked out well. I have always been a one friend guy, it's just easier that way.
Ralph lives in a row home in a lower class part of town. He grew up a bit different than I did. He dish-washed at a bar called Romano's at the end of the homes since he was 13. It wasn't even legal but they paid him under the

table. He finally quit last year when he couldn't get a raise and he works in a retirement home now.

I usually sit in his basement for a while and eat some pasta his mom makes. She's full blooded Italian and can barely speak English, it's kind of funny. She is constantly cooking and the whole place smells like an Italian restaurant. I try to turn her down sometimes, but she doesn't take no for an answer. Ralph's family does most of their living in the basement of the house for some reason. The upstairs looks like a museum with plastic on the old Italian furniture. After eating we usually play a little PlayStation or old school Nintendo while his dad sleeps in his chair with his stained white shirt.

2) Then Ronnie DeCamillo usually shows up with his white Dodge Neon.

Ronnie is a year older than us and is on the football team as well. He's not like a normal popular football player, he's a big dude that doesn't drink or go to parties or get chicks. That's not really his scene. Hence why he hangs with Ralph and me. Ronnie used to wash dishes at Romano's as well.

3) We bolt out of there once he shows up, and we drive around in Ronnie's car for a few hours not going anywhere in particular. There is really nowhere for us to go, so we just drive around and talk and make occasional stops at convenience stores. There isn't even pot or beer

involved. The point is just getting out of the house and away from everyone.

4) At least once a night we go to the all-night donut shop. Ronnie loves his donuts. The "Chocolate Thunder" donuts are his favorite. We make a game of it: he tries to inhale as many as he can by the time we get to the first traffic light half a mile down the street. His current record is five.

5) Around midnight Ronnie drops me off at home, and I will usually go to my room and watch a movie.

Kind of lame, huh? I think so. Compared to what I think the kids in my class are doing on the weekends, its super lame. Who knows, maybe they're driving around like we are. I doubt it though.

November 25, 1996

As time went on, lunch after lunch, I was slowly getting to know the real Darcy. She would let things slip at the lunch table, giving me little pieces of the puzzle of her life that I was secretly putting together.

Darcy is from a well off family. They aren't super rich but her dad is some type of business man, and they have a mini-mansion with a nice in-ground pool and a shore house. She doesn't see her dad that much though. Maybe that's why she acts out so much and dates these jerk off guys. I heard that girls with "daddy issues" acted wildly to try to get their fathers' attention. Who knows.

She doesn't talk about her older brother that much. I know he graduated from Lindsburg a few years ago and is still living at home. Apparently, he tried to go to community college, but flunked out. Now, he just lives at home and works part time at a pizza shop. That's all I know. Oh, and he buys her beer whenever she wants and Cecelia says that he hits on her all the time when she's over there. I'm pretty sure he deals weed on the side. Sounds like he has a nice life to me.

I wish my parents were rich. As long as I remember, we never had much money. My parents married young; both were 18 years old, right out of high school. My mom was pregnant with my older sister, Sarah, so they had to grow up quick. I'm 16 years old, and couldn't imagine having a child in two years. I can barely get to school and work. I just want to watch TV and play video games.

When my sister was 5, they had me, and then 3 years later they had my younger brother, Don. Everyone thought that would be our family, and, out of the blue, two years ago, my parents had my youngest brother, Steve. I don't know what they were thinking. They must really like raising kids. It must be a Catholic thing. Baby Steve doesn't bother me too much and I'm happy that I have my own room now that Sarah is in college. I stay in there most of the time.

Before Sarah went to college, I had to room with Don, and it was a nightmare. We were constantly fighting about everything. Thank God that's over. I don't talk to him much anymore. He seems like he's much cooler than I'm and he's into rap music. He's always telling me to turn down my classic rock; he hates it.

Even though we're poor, I'm used to living the way we do: eating macaroni and cheese, hotdogs, Encore microwavable dinners, buying clothes second hand, driving old junker station wagons, and going to flea markets. We have a pool but it's the above ground white trash version. The funny thing is, all of this felt perfectly normal to me until I got into high school. I was immediately exposed to kids who live in rich areas, like Darcy and most of the guys on the soccer team. It changed my whole view of the world.

I remember one day at soccer practice, the guys were all going around comparing cleats. They all had expensive brand name footwear like *Nike* and *Reebok* and when they got to me, Marshall Gomer looked at my beat up pair of no name brand cleats and said "What the hell are those?"

"*Alex* brand, I don't know; I got them at a garage sale for three bucks," I said.

"Hahaha," he laughed. "Holy shit, what is wrong with you Walenti?"

"I don't really care; they're just shoes."

"No wonder you can't get on the field!" he said loudly, looking around at everyone.

I felt like such a loser. I just wanted to fit in and I didn't know how. At that point I just wanted to go home. I almost quit after that, but I went home and told my mom. She took me out and we got a nice new pair of cleats the next day. It didn't matter, I still wasn't accepted. They had made up their mind.

November 27, 1996

One of the worst parts about school is taking the bus. Some kids get lucky and have older siblings, and they'll get a ride into school, like Ralph. Not me. I have to be out there at the bus stop at 6:15 in the morning. School starts at 7:45 so you would think I wouldn't have to get out there so early. The problem is that I'm the first stop. So I have an hour-and-a-half long bus ride to a school that's a 10 minute drive away. It's the worst. The only thing that's nice is getting on the bus and having all the seats available because I am the first to get in.

I remember the first day of school my freshman year. I walked to the bus stop across the street in another development and there were a bunch of public school kids there and one Lindsburg kid in a uniform. Thank God, at least I'm not the only one in a uniform, I thought. In grade school we had our own bus stop in our development, so I didn't have to worry about looking like a dork in my uniform around kids from other schools. I have to admit, the public school kids seemed terrifying in their normal clothes. It was a world that I never knew. I had been put in Catholic school in kindergarten.

When I got to the bus stop that first morning, the other Lindsburg kid looked at me and then turned away quickly. Apparently, he knew all the public school kids at the bus stop from his neighborhood, and he could tell that I was a loser with one look. He wanted nothing to do with me. So, I just stood there and waited, not talking to anyone.

It turned out that the guy at the bus stop was a

football player and he got popular really fast. A few months later, he was getting a ride from a senior football player and didn't have to take the bus anymore. I was glad when he wasn't there anymore. It was so awkward standing there in matching uniforms in front of the public school kids with nothing to say to him.

As a freshman, I played it safe and sat near the front. I didn't know any of the kids who would sit in the back, and I really didn't want to know them. Most of them were assholes who terrorized kids for no reason. I knew to be as far away as possible was my best bet.

I think their sadistic behaviors had to do with their family situation. I saw their houses and they lived in dilapidated row homes. I don't know how their parents afforded the tuition. It had to be a nightmare in those small homes at night with the fighting and yelling. They brought that anger to school and took it out on whoever they could.

My trick was to slink down in the seat as far as possible. You had to do this because they would throw shit at your head. It was a prime target. I had my Walkman, so I would just listen to tapes and look out the window until we got to school.

I have to put up with all this crap to go to a place that I don't want to go to. In four months and change and I'll be getting my license. Then, freedom - sweet sweet freedom...and an extra hour of sleep.

November 30, 1996

Thanksgiving is the stupidest holiday. We get a day off of school, and we have to spend all day with family. And there aren't even presents. What's the point? At least with Christmas, I come away from my mom-mom and pop-pops house with a haul of stuff. Even on Easter we get candy and money. Thanksgiving is just eating and waiting to go home.

This year, we had it at my aunt's house. It changes every year between our house, hers and my grand mom's. My aunts food is good, but everything has a different flavor, which I don't like. I prefer my mom's stuffing and mashed potatoes and the canned cranberry sauce. My aunt does fancy things with her food, and it never tastes right.

Also this year, my sister, Sarah, brought her college boyfriend to my aunt's house. He's this big muscular guy who's really tan, and looks like he was a really cool guy in high school. I think he's Italian. He reminds me of an ape. I thought he was going to be a dick but surprisingly he was a really nice guy, and now I don't mind him at all.

For as long as I can remember, my sister always had a boyfriend. She would switch them out without anyone knowing. She is five years older than me so when she was in high school, I was still in grade school. She would usually go out with them for a month or so and then all the sudden a new one would show up to the house. I never liked any of her boyfriends she had in high school except for this one guy, Casey. He had a cool Camaro, and even brought his Nintendo over and left it so we could play Super Mario Bros. 3 for a week! It was amazing.

They also have the Thanksgiving Day high school football game every year. It's a rivalry game we play against the closest public school to us, North Park High. The football players and pretty much the whole school makes a big deal about it. I don't understand it. I didn't go last year, and I certainly didn't go this year. I couldn't even tell you who won the game. I guess I'll find out on Monday. Even though I want to kick for the team someday, I don't feel welcome in the stands with all the popular kids. It's another place I don't belong. Those places outnumber the places I feel comfortable being.

I only went to one football game my freshman year. I didn't even want to go, but got roped into it by this kid, Dana Tisdal, who I didn't even like. He was already 16 as a freshman and had a car. He got held back twice during grade school, so he was obviously kind of dumb. His parents were super rich, and they gave him a brand new car. Since he was the first one in our grade with a car, girls would constantly use him for rides to and from school and to the mall and other stuff.

I felt bad for him, he's worse off than I am and the only reason anybody talked to him is because he could drive. People make fun of him behind his back because he has a girl's name and is freckled from head to toe and has dusty red curly hair. He looks like the fat kid catcher from *The Sandlot*.

Anyway, he picked up Ralph and me one night, and we were driving around with nothing to do. He said he wanted to go to the football game because some of the girls said they needed a ride home. So we went at halftime and stood in the stands for a while. All the cool kids were sitting in one section. They were all cheering and having fun. We just stood there and pretended to watch the game. None of us cared who won. It was really awkward, and we couldn't wait until it was over.

At the end of the game, Ralph and I went out to the car. Dana went to go to talk to the girls who wanted a ride. They told him that they were headed to a party with some other people and didn't need his car. They didn't even invite him to the party. He came walking back to the car alone; then, we went to a diner and got some cheese fries. That was how most nights ended our freshman year.

I feel bad for Dana now. Since more and more kids are getting their licenses, the girls aren't talking to him anymore. His usefulness has expired. They are so evil.

December 2, 1996

So I've been kicking for a few weeks now. Every day after school, I get out and kick the ball against the shed. I'm actually getting better. My foot doesn't hurt anymore, and I barely kick up dirt. My kicks are mostly clean and I'm getting good power. I wanted to see how far I could kick it so I rode my bike to an old baseball field at a church down the street. My dad used to take us there to practice as kids, and I never saw anybody there. It's back away from the road, which is what I wanted. I couldn't suffer the humiliation of people driving by and seeing me kick a football over a backstop.

It was cold out that day at around 30 degrees. The field was frozen solid. I thought about *Rocky IV* when he was training in Russia in the snow. I love that movie. I love all of the Rockys except the last one. The first one is by far the best though. I think I've seen it over 10 times. Growing up near Philadelphia, it's a staple.

Most people think *Rocky I* is a sports/action movie but it's not. It's really a touching love story. The movie starts with him as this really lonely guy who has nothing and with the help of his girlfriend, he gains the confidence to go toe to toe with the heavyweight boxing champion of the world. Just thinking about it right now, I can hear the theme music in my head, and it gives me chills.

Out there in the cold, I lined up my first kick and gave it a good whack. The ball was frozen and felt more like hard plastic than rubber. It went up in the air about half way up the chain link baseball backstop. My foot kind of stung after the kick. I think I was trying too hard. The next kick I relaxed and kicked it like I normally did, and it went right over. I was only 20 yards away, but it was good that I got the height. That was what I was most worried about. I stayed out there for about 45 minutes. I didn't stand back very far. My focus was more to see if I could get it over the backstop and I did. Height was important.

I rode my bike back home with a big smile on my

face for the first time in a long time.

Rocky IV: 4/5 stars (even though I haven't seen it in ages)

Rocky I: 5/5 stars

December 3, 1996

I never had a shot with Darcy from the beginning. When you start high school, there is about a week or two of acclimation during which you can assimilate with anybody you want. It's pretty much a fresh start. Lindsburg isn't like public school, where you know mostly the same kids through all 12 years of school. There are a bunch of Catholic grade schools around the area and after 8th grade, all the students dump into Lindsburg Catholic.

So, as a freshman, you can find a bunch of new friends to hang with, and most of the girls don't know who you are. I'm so shy that I didn't reach out to anybody. I just stuck to hanging out with Ralph and didn't make any attempt to make some new friends. I'm bad like that. I like my comfort zone, and unless I'm pushed out of it, I stay there. It sucks.

Darcy started dating her boyfriend when she was a freshman. He was two years older and already a varsity baseball player. Even though she was relatively unknown for the first couple of weeks, I never made a move to talk to her. Then, there was the first big party of the year, which I of course was not at, and I heard she got really drunk and hooked up with two guys. After that, she was on the radar as a "fun girl." The upperclassmen were like wolves. When they heard this kind of stuff, they all started to put the moves on her.

Eventually, she picked the best of the bunch, Matt Reinhart, the star junior baseball player who came at her hard.

I sat a few seats away from her in history class, and she would come in on Mondays and talk to her friend Jenna who sat right near me about her weekend and the different places she would hook up with Matt with her friend Jenna who sat right near me. It usually involved them in the basement of somebody's house, or a in car, and even in the woods one time. It was crazy what I was hearing. She didn't even seem bashful about it.

I wasn't that crushed about it back then, because she seemed so out of my league, but thinking about it now, I get kind of sad. It's mostly because I talk to her now and think I have shot, which is completely delusional.

Darcy and Cecilia are pretty much attached at the hip. They've been a package deal since freshman year. Apparently they lived in the same neighborhood when they were kids, and were friends their whole lives. They were very different though. As Darcy is pretty, reckless and kind of an extrovert, Cecilia is a little chunky, a straight A student and didn't open her mouth that much. It is a strange relationship.

It was rare that they kept up a friendship like that. I knew girls who were friends all through grade school, and then as soon as high school started, they drifted apart. Especially if one was hotter than the other. I wonder if Darcy keeps Cecilia by her side because she makes her look better. I know for a fact that Cecilia does her homework for her sometimes and gives her test answers.

It would make sense if I asked out Cecilia but I don't think she's that hot. I don't understand why loser guys like me are attracted to dangerous girls who are out of our league. It doesn't make sense. We know that even if we get them that they will get bored with us, yet we still can't stop drooling. Ugggh!

December 4, 1996

My English teacher, Mr. Leyland, is one of my favorite teachers. Not many people like him because he has a difficult personality. I remember him coming in the first day of sophomore year and reeking of cigarettes. I sat in the 3rd row and could smell him from there. Ralph said Mr. Leyland and his older brother, who graduated a few years ago, would smoke butts behind the school, back in the day. That made me like him even more.

He is like no teacher I ever had. He speaks to us as adults, which really blows my mind. He made it a rule to address everyone in the class by Mr. or Ms., such as "Yes Mr. Walenti, what is the answer?" or "Yes Ms. Reynolds, you must have something to add."

He loved Ms. Reynolds. Lilly Reynolds is this cute short blond girl who was never the focus of the boys attention in grade school, but something happened over the summer from 8th to 9th grade: She grew enormous breasts. It was crazy. She was already petite so this made her insanely hot. She knows this and loves walking around the hallways with her chest proudly stuck out.

It's dumb luck that her alphabetically assigned seat is dead center in front of Mr. Leyland.

Mr. Leyland always has a scowl on his face when teaching the class and you could tell he's a miserable man. I think is because he is divorced. He's always telling us to wait until we are in our 30's to get married. I often wonder what happened to him. I imagine he was happy at some point in his life and then his wife left him and ever since then he's been bitter. Or maybe he's just always been miserable and his wife couldn't take it anymore. Making up stories about people is my way of getting though the day. It's kind of like a game to me, like I am writing my own TV show in my head.

I guess Mr. Leyland's misery is why he smokes so much. Who knows? I have never smoked so I have no idea what it is like. All I know is that whenever I see him out there smoking, he seems happy and content. Another thing that does make him smile is when Lilly Reynold's raises her hand. "Yes Ms. Reynolds, how are you today," he would say. It is pretty creepy and everyone can tell he likes her, but he never does anything wrong, so he never gets in any trouble.

He would always assign us book reports on Greek Mythology, which was actually kind of interesting with all the gods and the monsters. I loved reading those stories compared to the boring Bible. But the strange thing was that he would never collect the reports. This went on for about a month. Every week we would get assigned a report on a different chapter, and it would be two pages long. I didn't understand why he wasn't collecting the reports. "No, I trust you did them, we are all adults in this class," he would say and then would have kind of an evil smirk on his face.

So, by the end of the first month, nobody was doing the reports anymore because he wasn't collecting them, not even me. I always followed the rules and never wanted to be in trouble, but it seemed pointless to waste my time writing something that wouldn't be graded.

On Monday, he brought down the axe. He came in, looked around the room, and then announced

"Everyone pass your latest book reports to the front, I'm going to grade them."

WHAT THE HELL? I thought.

Everyone was stunned. Not one person in the class had done their paper, except Lilly Reynolds. Lilly gave hers to the teacher, and he stared at us for about a minute not saying anything.

"Why has no one done their report except for Ms. Reynolds? I thought we had a level of adult trust in this classroom," he said in a sarcastic tone.

The classroom was silent. I looked down at my desk and was glad I wasn't the only one who didn't do the paper.

"Seems like you have all let me down, so I have to punish all of you except for Ms. Reynolds," he said.

"You will all go home tonight and write out the entire fifth chapter in the Greek Mythology book on paper. No typing; it's due on Wednesday."

The class erupted in huge screams and sighs. We were defeated; he set up an elaborate trap probably just for his own enjoyment. Did he tell Ms. Reynolds about his plan? She was a quiet girl who didn't associate with a lot of people, so I don't know if she was in on it or she just did her homework every week and got lucky. It was crazy. Chapter 5 was 26 pages long!

I went home that night, sat in my room, and actually wrote out the 26 pages all day. I didn't quite finish so I woke up early and was able to finish by 3rd period. Luckily English was at the end of the day. When we walked in today, almost everyone had done the punishment, except a few of the burnouts who didn't even care. He walked in and proceeded to teach class without mentioning the punishment at all. At the end of class, we asked him if he wanted our papers, and he just replied "No, what am I going to do with them, I have the book, I probably can't read your handwriting anyway. Just throw them in the garbage on the way out."

AAAAAHHHHHHHHH!!!

December 8, 1996

I was hanging in Ralph's basement the other day, and a really cheesy/cool movie came on cable. It's called *Lock Up* and stars Sylvester Stallone. It came out in the 80's and is about a guy who is framed for a crime and gets put into prison. I didn't get to see the beginning but Ralph had seen it already and filled me in about what it was about.

For some reason, the warden, played by Donald Sutherland, is out to get him. He hates Stallone's character. They like to make the wardens in prison movies really evil characters. Sometimes it works, like in *Shawskank Redemption*, and sometimes it doesn't, like in this movie. That's ok though; *Lock up* is pure 80's popcorn garbage. That means you just watch it and enjoy, you don't look at it like a good movie; it's just entertaining.

The best part is when they actually fix up a 1965 Ford Mustang in the prison! I don't even know how that would be possible, but they did it in a 3-5 minute montage. I love movie montages; so much gets done in such a short time. They even played a cool song in the montage called *Vehicle*, by Ides of March. I didn't recognize the song, but Ralph's brother, Vince, knew it right away. I had heard it on the radio before and always liked it.

At the end of the montage, they have a bright red fully restored mustang in the prison garage. How did they get the parts? Why did the warden let them do this? None of that mattered. It was the 80's.

The car ends up getting destroyed when the one guy takes it out for a drive in the prison yard. That was when the warden decided to get his revenge.

It was a ridiculous movie but I enjoyed it. It sucked though, because all the curse words were bleeped out. I hate movies on TBS; the commercials and the censored words make it almost unwatchable.

Whatever, it was free.

Lock Up: 2.5/5 stars

December 10, 1996

The Winter Dance is coming up. I hate the Winter Dance almost more than the prom. Last year it was called the Christmas Dance but I guess they changed it for political correctness since not all kids celebrate Christmas. Even though it's a Catholic School, we have a bunch of Protestants, Jewish, and non-religious kids. Most of them came from families with money, and their parents didn't want them going to public school.

I hate all dances or so I think. I've never been to a dance so I can only assume they're terrible. On second thought, I guess I don't hate dances, just the people that go to them. Our group of misfits doesn't even talk about going to dances; there's no point. Our school is small, so there aren't many options, date-wise. The hot girls either went out with the jocks, or the stoners. Everything else in between was scary. I'm not saying that I'm anything to look at but some of the girls are downright homely.

My football friend, Jerry Romano, goes to the dances, but he's part of the social elite, so it makes sense for him to go. Jerry is the starting linebacker for the football team and all around social butterfly. He loves walking around the hallways talking to everyone. I don't know how he does it.

I met Jerry through Ralph. They grew up together and it was just dumb luck that they were friends. Jerry's dad owned the bar Romano's near Ralph's house so they both washed dishes there with Ronnie and all three of them are lifelong friends. In any other world there's no way a guy like Jerry would talk to me or Ralph. We are definitely secondary friends though, that's certain. Jerry has his core of football buds, and he hangs out with us when nothing else is going on. That's fine, it's better than nothing.

I could have gone to a dance with a girl last year. This really ugly girl Linda Deluke asked me to the end of the year Freshman Dance. Linda was overweight and had a ton of acne on her face. I wasn't even expecting it; she blindsided me. I didn't even know her, and she came up to my locker and asked me to the dance. I was freaked out and just made up some excuse about not being able to go. I don't even remember what I said.

Later on, I felt bad for her. In a perfect world, I would have taken her to the dance and not cared what people thought. In the real world, if I had taken her, I would have put a "loser" spotlight on myself for the rest of high school. I couldn't do that.

I had it bad in school but I had it better than being a girl like Linda. The girls in high school are so brutal. They tease each other nonstop so bad. If you're an ugly girl, they let you know it. At least as a nerdy guy I'm left alone. These hot girls walk around the hallways like they own the place. I heard a good saying on TV the other "He acts like his shit don't stink," which really describes how those girls act. It wasn't enough for these girls to have everything they ever wanted but they felt the need to punish the underlings. They would stand around their lockers and cackle like hyenas making fun of the girls with pimples, lump rolls, and weird faces. Yet, I still wanted to date them. That is why I like Darcy. She never did any of that. She stayed in her lane and didn't bully any of them.

That girl, Linda, ended up transferring out after freshman year. I have no clue where she went. Nobody really said anything about her leaving. Nobody; she was more invisible than I was.

I still think about her. She is the only girl that ever asked me out, which is kind of sad now that I think about it.

December 15, 1997

I was watching the Philadelphia Eagles today with my dad, and I saw the kicker, Chris Boniol, do something I hadn't noticed before. Right before he starts to go towards the ball, he does a small stutter step with his left leg. I thought it was mistake the first time but he kept doing it. I changed the channel to another game, and the kickers in that game were doing it too! So weird. After the game was over, I went out and tried it, and it didn't really change how I kicked. So, I don't know why they do this but I'm going to do it because there has to be some reason for it. Maybe Jerry knows.

December 18, 1996

I wish I started this journal last year. There was so much I could have written about. Like when I was 15, I bought a 1972 El Camino for 400 bucks. An El Camino is this funky old car that is a mix between a car and truck. It was in pretty bad shape, but I was excited to have something to fix up. I didn't know anything about cars, but my dad did. He had been fixing them since he was in high school, so he said he would give me a hand. It ran well but the body was in pretty bad shape.

I got the car last winter so I would go out in the garage on a Friday night with my Walkman and my mix-tape of rock music. I couldn't afford a Discman or CD's so I would wait by the radio with a blank cassette ready to go. When a good song came on the radio, like *Basket Case* by Green Day, I would hit record and capture the song on the tape. Then I would wait around for another song to come on, and that's how I made my mix tapes. Most of freshman year I sat at home on Friday nights when radio stations played rock blocks of Led Zeppelin, Metallica, Black Sabbath, The Who, Nirvana, Alice in Chains and Guns and Roses. I loved all rock music, especially the classic stuff.

It was nice out there in the garage alone with my classic car and my music. I would turn on my dad's big kerosene heater and make the garage all nice and warm before I would start on the body work. I would go to town sanding and filling in the holes with body putty. It would have been nice to replace the body parts with new metal, but I was a poor high school kid and I still am, so the cheap putty was the only way to go. Those nights, I didn't care what any of my classmates were doing. They could have their parties and dances; I was doing something they weren't.

It was worth it. By the summertime, my car was all painted up nice a nice metallic blue and ready for a driver with a license. It is so hard seeing it there in the driveway and not being able to drive it. Three more months or so until I turn 16!

December 20, 1996

Christmas is my favorite time of year. We get a full week off of school and the weather is cold, so it's the ultimate excuse to stay inside and play video games.

The only downside is that my sister Sarah is home for a whole month. She was only around for a few days for Thanksgiving but now she's stuck home until Spring semester start's up sometime in mid-January.

I was playing my new PlayStation game *Twisted Metal* last night, and she and my mom were yelling back and forth.

"I want you back home at midnight," my mom said.

"No, I'm an adult now and shouldn't have a curfew." Sarah said.

"What time are you coming home?"

"I don't know, I might sleep over Rob's house."

"Oh no, when you're living here, you abide by our rules!" my mom yelled.

"I hate you!" Sarah shouted back.

She ran out of the house, and I continued to play my game.

I don't understand why they argue so much. It's like they feed off each other. I never argue with my parents; it seems like too much work. I just keep quiet and follow the rules. I guess that's why I don't get anywhere with girls. They want dangerous outspoken guys who get them excited. Maybe I'll be that one day, probably not though.

December 25, 1996

I made out pretty good this year. I got some new PlayStation games, some nice tools, some cassette tapes from my sister: Alice in Chains–*Facelift,* Pearl Jam–*Ten,* and a bunch of money from my aunts, uncles, and grandparents. It was worth all the punishment of dressing up, going to church and then going to my grand moms with my cousins.

I was so happy to get home and listen to the Alice in Chains tape on my Walkman. They had such a cool sound like nothing I've ever heard before. I need to save my money for a Disc-Man though; it's such a pain to have to rewind and fast forward to find the song I want to listen to. Disc-man's are so damn expensive though, the good Sony one is over 100 bucks!

At least this year we were able to open our presents before church. Last year, my parents wanted to try something new and wait until after church to open them. It was excruciating, sitting there in church bored as hell wondering what was in those boxes. I know I'm getting old for Christmas but getting free shit rules. I can barely afford anything on my McDonald's check, so I have to take what I can get.

December 28, 1996

I was sitting at Ralph's house on Friday night, and he got a call from Jerry. Jerry told him to meet him outback in the alley; he was picking us up to go out. This was always exciting, because we never knew what he had up his sleeve. Ralph and I would usually sit around and watch movies or play video games on Friday nights, so when Johnny asked us to hang out, we always said yes.

Ralph told his mom he was going out, and she yelled "Where you going?" in broken English. "Don't worry about it!" he shouted back.

We got in the car, and he drove out of the alley.

"Where are we going?" Ralph asked.

"Here, hit this, you guys need to mellow." Jerry said handing him a glass bowl full of weed and a lighter.

Ralph took a hit and then handed it back to me. I took a small hit and then handed it to Jerry. I was glad I wasn't driving. Whenever I get high and have to drive, I get so paranoid about cops behind the car. I think every car is the police.

We drove around for a while just smoking and listening to the new Eminem album, The Slim Shady LP.

I didn't listen to much rap music, but when I was high, it seeped into my brain. I really liked that.

I told you, I pretty much hate rap, but Eminem is different. He's a white rapper who sounds completely ridiculous. He's so angry and he raps about off the wall stuff like drugs and doing horrible stuff to women. It's in a funny tone though; you can tell he isn't serious.

Jerry pulled into the grocery store and we staggered out into the fluorescent lights of the place. I didn't even know what we were doing there. Once I was in there, all I knew was that I needed some Doritos. Ralph and I went to the chip section while Jerry went off somewhere else. Being high in public freaked me out. I was positive the people in the store knew I was high and were staring at me. I was always looking around waiting for the cops to come in and take me to jail. I was better in the back seat of the car listening to music or in a room with some people on a bean bag chair.

We met Jerry at the checkout and he had a dozen roses and some condoms.

"What the fuck are you doing with that?" Ralph asked with a huge smile on his face.

"Playa's gotta play," Jerry said.

Where did he come up with these sayings? Must be all the rap music he listens to, I thought.

We drove around some more and kept smoking. A half hour later, Jerry pulled into a ritzy neighborhood with big houses and nice cars.

"Where the hell are we?" I asked.

"I'll be back in 20," Jerry said taking the flowers and the condoms.

"Whose house is this?" I asked Ralph.

"I'm pretty sure this is Katie Polk's house," he said.

"No way!" I screamed. "Holy shit!"

Katie Polk is a bombshell blond swimmer who turned heads since the first day of school. She had the biggest boobs in the class, even bigger than Lilly Reynold's, and all the guys were obsessed with her. I had never seen anything like her. I remember I sat behind her in freshman history class and you could see her bra right through the back of her shirt. What a sight! It seemed unfathomable that Jerry was in there with her.

Ralph and I sat in the car like a bunch of chumps while Johnny went in and did god knows what with that girl. At least he left us the keys, so we could listen to the music. A few minutes went by and then a light turned on upstairs and then flicked off. A half hour later, Jerry came strolling out and got in the car. He yelled "yeaaaa buddy!" and threw some panties at Ralph.

"What the fuck!" Ralph says.

"Dude, you stole them?" I said.

"Shiiiiit, that's just what I do," he says peeling away.

Jerry is such a cool guy. I can barely look at girls, and here he was driving up to their houses and getting sex like a drive thru. I'll never have that kind of confidence. Even though he acted cocky, I still liked to hang out with him. It was like a portal into the world of cool people. He shared stories with us about who was dating who and what went on at parties. He was living the dream that we wanted. He was Co-captain of the football team, starting linebacker and he could pretty much get any girl he wanted. He was the exact opposite of Ralph and me.

"Yea, I gave her the dirty bird behind the stage last week. She loves hooking up at school." Jerry said.

Ralph threw the panties back to me. It was the first time I held a pair of women's underwear. They were lacey pink panties, like the kind I saw in the bra and panty ads in the Sears Catalog. I just held them for a few seconds and then threw them up to Jerry because I felt weird holding them. He picked them up and put them right into his nose while he drove.

"Dude, you are a sick fuck!" Ralph said.

"You would be doing the same thing if you could," Jerry said.

He was right.

January 1, 1997

Happy New Year! I am one year closer to graduating and getting the hell out of this crappy school. I can't wait. Another dismal New Year's Eve spent doing nothing. Last night I hung out at Ralph's, and then we went over to Romano's bar because Chuck, Jerry's younger brother, was working in the kitchen.

Chuck is pretty much the exact opposite of Jerry. Jerry is outgoing, athletic, and popular, Chuck is not interested in sports or dances or anything except smoking pot. He picked up the habit in eighth grade and never stopped. Eighth grade! When I was riding my bike and playing video games, which I *still* do, he was smoking weed! He loves it. He woke up and smoked before school every day since then. After a while, he was just high all the time and you couldn't even tell anymore, it is his natural setting.

Chuck is a funny guy though; he's always creating new ways to smoke. One time, he put weed in an apple, and another time, he used a Pepsi can. I told him that I heard that smoking out of an aluminum can would give you Alzheimer's. He didn't seem to care. He said that one day he was going to invent a self-lighting bowl. That's his dream. He doesn't have many aspirations other than smoking weed, listening to rap and hooking up with girls.

I can't blame him. He probably isn't going to college, because his dad is going to give him the Romano's bar when he dies. So his future is laid out for him. I wish my parents had a business. I really don't want to go to college; I have had enough of school. I just want to get away from everyone. I can't even begin to think about what I'm going to do with my life. It seems so far away.

Chuck is like Jerry in a way though. He has his group of freshman friends and would only hang out with Ralph and me when he didn't have anything else to do.

It was kind of cool hanging out in the kitchen of a bar. All the waitresses are really hot and older, and they had half shirts on, so you could see their belly buttons. It's strange how guys find it hot when a woman shows off her belly button. The whole bar was super crowded, and people were getting really drunk. Romano's was kind of a dive bar, so it was mostly middle-aged losers who work blue collar jobs or don't work at all. It had its regular customers who literally drank there every day.

It wasn't the normal quiet sad bar on New Years; instead everyone was in a happy mood. Almost the whole place had on some sort of goofy New Year's hat or glasses or beads. Chuck would reserve one table for himself to sit and drink iced tea when the kitchen got slow, so we would sit with him and watch all the drunks. Seeing how stupid they looked made me not want to drink. I never really got drunk before. I had three beers once and started to feel it, but then I got nauseous and stopped. I was paranoid I would go home, and my parents would smell it. Then I would be in big trouble.

After the ball dropped, Chuck closed the kitchen, and we went over to his grand mom's basement which was right next door to the bar. His creepy 45 year old uncle lives there and he smokes pot with us, so we went over there and hung out until about 3:00 in the morning.

We just sat there, smoked pot, and watched a movie called *Reservoir Dogs*. Ralph and Chuck had seen it, but I hadn't. All I can say is, "WOW!" I freaking loved the film and plan on watching it again because I missed parts, because we were talking, and I was really high. It was great though, some of the scenes were so twisted. What I liked most about the movie was the dialogue. It was unlike anything I ever heard before. Now I have to watch *Pulp Fiction*, which is by the same director. I can't think of his name right now. I hear it's even better than *Reservoir Dogs*.

Yup, another New Years gone by and all I can say is that I watched another good movie. People on camera doing cool shit me *just* watching is my life summarized.

Reservoir Dogs: 4 / 5 stars (It would have gotten 5 stars but I missed a bunch of stuff. I'll go back and watch someday and reevaluate it.)

January 3, 1997

Darcy came into lunch crying today. I knew exactly why. I heard earlier in the day that Matt had cheated on her with Penelope Alverez, the Spanish foreign exchange student.

Penelope just showed up one day and made her mark immediately. At barely 5 feet tall and weighing 100 pounds with flowing black hair down to her ass, she walked those halls like she owned the place. Even the football players were intimidated. Such exotic beauty had never been seen in our boring white school.

It took about a week before anyone talked to Penelope, but once the seal was broken, there was no stopping her. She could have anyone she wanted. That first party she went to, I heard through the grapevine that she let some guys take body shots out of her belly button. I didn't even know you could do that. It sounded amazing. Her locker was five lockers away from mine, and she didn't even know I existed.

As Darcy cried, Cecelia put her arm around her and asked what happened.

"Matt fucked that whore Penelope!" she said loudly, not caring who heard.

"Fuck him, I hope he gets herpes from her," Cecilia said.

I sat there and ate my sandwich, not knowing what to do. I wanted to say I was sorry, and that I knew Matt was an asshole and I would gladly take his place as her boyfriend, but I just scarfed down a few chips followed by Cherry Coke. I really wanted to shout at her. I had seen this coming from a mile away.

A few weeks prior I had seen Matt and Penelope talking at her locker. It started with a few "hi's"as he walked by but then one day he stopped and engaged her. I knew it was trouble but I couldn't say anything to Darcy. If nothing happened, then it would look like I was trying to cause trouble.

In the end, it was better that it happened. Darcy finally saw him for who he was: a good looking, dumb baseball player with all the options in the world.

Eventually, she calmed down and just sat there looking at the table. She couldn't eat.

"Hey Darcy!" Greg yelled from across the table.

"What?" she asked still teary eyed, and kind of annoyed.

"We all decided that if you give us 100 bucks we can run Matt over with my car," he said sarcastically.

"Oh god!" she laughed a little and then ate a French fry. I think Greg is on the autistic spectrum or something because he has no filter and is good at breaking tension.

"No, what you really want to do is drain the oil out of his car without him knowing it. Then when he starts it, bam! The whole engine will seize." I said.

"That is so evil, I love it!" she said.

By the end of the lunch, she was feeling better, and we had her talking and laughing like always. I could tell she was still ripped up inside. She really loved that jerkoff. And I really love her. What a mess. How is anyone happy…ever?

January 5, 1997

On Saturday, Chuck took us to this head shop in Philly to look at weed pipes and bongs. He had been talking about going for a while, and I was curious. I had never been to one of those stores before so I was excited. The whole way there, Chuck smoked. First, it was a blunt, and then he packed a bowl when he was coming down. I stopped after a few puffs of the blunt because I was so high, and my mouth was so dry. I'm a lightweight. Not him. He kept on going and going.

When we got there, I went into the store and everything was tilty. Like the room was askew. The place was weird, and the people in there were strange. It was like going back to the 60's. They had tapestries all over the wall and ceiling, and incense was burning. I just walked around and looked at all the bongs and cool glass pipes. They were all colorful and some had animal designs.

Chuck picked out a really nice 1 foot glass bong and bought it for 60 dollars. I wanted to buy my own pipe, but I was worried my parents might find it, so I didn't. Then I saw the cashier get a box out from under the counter and ring it up.

"What's in the box?" I asked.

"Nitrous," Chuck said.

"What is that?"

"You'll see."

In the car he pulled off the lid, and there were a ton of little silver canisters all lined up. Chuck put one in some contraption he called a "cracker," and then sucked on the end.

"Oh fuck," he said, and then he started laughing like a fool.

Ralph went next, and then he was laughing. Chuck had stopped laughing by the time Ralph sucked one down.

"Here," Chuck said as he loaded the cracker. Just crack and suck.

"What does it feel like?"

"Heaven."

"How long does it last?"

"20 seconds."

"Oh, ok."

I cracked the canister and sucked it down. The rest of the experience was pure bliss. All my problems were gone. It actually did feel like heaven. I started laughing like they did and thought everything was going to be ok. Then the feeling went away after 15 seconds, and I felt like a real dummy. I actually felt dumber. How many brain cells did I just kill?

Chuck and Ralph continued to pass the nitrous back and forth on the ride home. It was really dangerous that Chuck was driving and doing that stuff.

I wanted to yell at him, but I just laid down in the back and hoped we got home ok.

We did. And the whole case was gone as well. They huffed it all.

January 10, 1997

I didn't think it could get better than *Reservoir Dogs*. I was wrong. *Pulp Fiction* is a fantastic movie. I found out the director's name is Quintin Tarantino and he is kind of a genius.

Pulp Fiction is the same style as *Reservoir Dogs,* but it's a more complete movie. There are a ton more characters, and they all don't know each other but end up crossing paths at some point in the movie. It's genius.

Their time lines are all over the place, and it was hard to follow the first time around. I watched it 2 times in one night because I was kind of confused the first time.

After the second time, it all came together. It was such a layered story, I wonder how someone could write something like that. It must have taken a long time.

Pulp Fiction: 5/5 stars (*Reservoir Dogs* still stays at 4; this movie blows it away, and I can't put both of them at 5 for some reason I can't explain).

January 13, 1997

Our school is so lame. I can't believe my parents spend 3,000 dollars a year to send me here. I watch TV shows where public school kids are taking shop class, and it looks so fun. I love working with tools; why can't we have that? Oh yea, our school is too cheap. We don't have anything that public schools have: home economics, a swimming pool, a football stadium, a vo-tech program, and probably a ton of other things I don't know about because I never set foot in a public school. I would love to be in a classroom full of girls baking a cake. What the fuck!

Oh, and they don't have to wear uniforms! Now that I'm thinking about it, that last one is actually good. I don't have to think about wearing cool clothes on a daily basis. Also the girls wearing skirts is a huge, huge advantage over public school. Some of the girls hike them up really high, and Mr. Girard yells at them to pull their skirts down. Sometimes you hear about a slutty girl not wearing underwear and they will also get in trouble. I don't know what they're thinking, but I think it's kind of cool.

We do have "dress down days" about once a month, when the school lets us wear our normal clothes for a day, usually on a Friday. They even make us pay a dollar. I do feel a great amount of anxiety trying to pick something out people won't make fun of. The football team wears their jerseys, even when the season is over, the whores try to get away with mid-drift shirts and short skirts, and the stoners wear skater jeans and long shirts. The rest of us just stick to normal clothes: jeans, t-shirt and sneakers.

The worst is when you forget that it's dress down day and show up with your uniform on. I did that last year and when I got to the bus stop I suddenly remembered it was dress down day. I tried to run back and change but the bus was a few houses away.

It's interesting to see what the girls look like out of their uniforms. They are like different people. There is definitely a new energy in the school when we get to wear normal clothes. Kids act out more and are all riled up. Those uniforms really do wear us down like we are in some dystopian movie and all have to wear the same clothes; it breaks most of our spirits and helps us fall in line. The truly maniacal kids don't care either way, they fuck shit up regardless.

January 15, 1997

In health class I sit right behind Mackenzie Wilco. She's this girl who has long black curly hair and wears black lipstick. She looks like such a badass, more so than Darcy. She sits next to Alissa Cayland, another girl who's super-hot and super skinny who wears black lipstick as well.

I overheard them talking today and apparently Mackenzie is dating some college guy. She talks about how he picks her up down the street from her parents' house and then takes her to his nearby college where they have sex in his dorm room. The guy must be such a loser to be dating a 16 year old girl. First it's illegal and second, why can't he get a college girl? I wonder how they even met. How does anyone get together? It seems impossible for me.

Mackenzie and Alissa are those type of girls who think they're cooler than everyone. They act like they don't care about anything but I know they do. I can tell because of the way they wear black lipstick, cool punk music patches on their backpacks and the black outfits from Hot Topic on dress down day. In reality, they care a whole lot. Those outfits take a long time to put together, so obviously they want people to think they're rebels. I'm the one who doesn't care, pretty much about anything, yet here I am, just taken for granted.

I should really change my look. It would be too hard though. Everyone would look at me that first day and I would feel like an idiot. I'm stuck with this image for the rest of high school. Maybe in college I can come up with some fake identity; nobody will know me there. It would be a fresh start. That's why I need to make this kicking thing happen. I have to; it's my last chance to make my mark at this school.

By the way, health class is really dumb. I don't understand why they have the gym teacher, Mr. Hollister, teach the class. He doesn't know anything. He's some meathead who barely graduated college with a degree in Physical Education. What the hell is that? Did he have to take classes in dodgeball and floor hockey? Why do you even need a college degree to be a gym teacher?

When he shows us STD's on the projector, I want

to throw up. Some people ask questions about them and he usually doesn't know the answer. He writes them down and says he'll answer the next class. I guess the school is strapped for money so they can't hire a good health teacher.

It doesn't even matter though. He shows us how to eat and exercise, and nobody cares. At lunch, we scarf down soda and pizza and fries. He shows us these disgusting images of what sexually transmitted diseases like syphilis can do to your brain, and it doesn't stop my classmates from hooking up non-stop. He shows us what happens when you smoke and what a black lung looks like, and the cool kids still smoke before and after school. Nothing they say will stop kids from doing what they want. Don't they understand that?

January 16, 1997

Before study hall today, Martin Kerr was talking about how he was getting together some people for a party at his parents shore house on Saturday. Martin is easily one of the most known kids in our grade. He's a really good guitar player, plays ice hockey, and is friends with a bunch of the stoners. His dad owns a company that prints paper materials for businesses, like pamphlets and stuff. They're upper middle class, like Darcy. They also have a huge house and an expensive shore house in Ocean City, NJ.

I had heard about his parties in the past. He would go down there in the winter when the whole town was abandoned and they would just drink a ton of beer and smoke pot. It sounded like so much fun. I still can't believe his parents let him do that. There's no way my parents would let me have a party here or at the shore or anywhere.

I sometimes work at Martin's dad's company on the weekend because my mom is a secretary there. Whenever they get busy I help them out for "under the table" money. That's when they just give you cash. I love that. My McDonald's check is a joke after they take out the taxes. Martin is there sometimes working, and we talk about school and *The Simpsons*. It is strange, we get along so well there, but then at school he doesn't really talk to me. Martin does acknowledge me when I walk by but there is never any talk of hanging out after school. I guess since no one from school is around at his dad's company, it's ok to talk to a loser like me.

So before study hall today, Martin and a couple of the other ice hockey players are talking about the party at the shore house. I sit a table away and was listening to them bust balls and talk about chicks and beer and weed. Then Darcy came in, and then Martin yelled "Yo Darcy, party next week at the shore house."

"Nice! I'm down. I think we should get Nic drunk," she says.

"Haha, yea. Walenti, you wanna come down?" Martin asks.

"Fuck yea, sounds like fun." I said. I started to internally freak out after that. It was excitement and then nervousness.

"Oh man, you think you can handle this? I've never seen you at a party." Darcy said.

"I'll be fine, don't you worry." I said with fake confidence.

The bell rang to start study hall and Mr. Donner yelled. I sat there the rest of the period dreaming of a drunken single Darcy. This was my shot!

January 22, 1997

Wow, the last few days have been crazy. I feel like a celebrity! I have so much to talk about.

On Saturday we left for the shore around 1:00 pm. I rode down with Martin and a couple of the hockey guys. They had a whole trunk full of beer and a few bottles of liquor, mostly vodka, rum and whiskey. I figured I would stick to beer to be on the safe side. I didn't really like the taste of beer, but the few times that I've had it, the feeling of being drunk was like nothing else. I smelled vodka before, and it's disgusting. It was like rubbing alcohol. Why would anyone want to drink that?

I was so nervous about going. This was something totally out of character for me. Nobody ever invited me to something like this. The days leading up to the party, I started chewing on my fingers non-stop. This is something I've been doing my whole life. I don't know why either. Normal people chew their fingernails, but I chew the skin around my fingers when I'm nervous.

Most of the time, I don't even know I'm doing it.

When I was a kid, and my mom caught me, I stopped for a while and then chewed the collar of my shirt until it was totally gone. It is a curse; I hat it because my thumb knuckles get all scabbed and bloody after a while. It was only then that I stopped until they healed, and then I would started up again.

During the car ride down Martin and the guys were all smoking cigarettes. They offered me one, but I said no. I never smoked a cigarette and it scared me to get think I could get addicted to something. I was already addicted to TV and movies; I didn't need something else. Also, it would be really hard to hide smoking from my parents; the smell takes over your whole body. I know, because I can smell Mr. Leyland from the back of the classroom.

I was feeling cooler than I ever had by just being in the car with them. It felt like I won the lottery.

When we got to the house, we unloaded all the beer and food and waited for the other people to show up. Martin was kind of in the middle of the jocks and stoners, so he had invited a little of both.

Mackenzie Wilco and Alissa Cayland walked in the door, each with a bottle in their hand. They both were wearing skirts and black panty hose. They looked so hot. Rumor was that Martin was hooking up with Alissa. This was the first time I had seen them outside of school. They saw me on the couch and I saw the look on their faces. That look of "what are you doing here?"

I started with a beer. It tasted awful, so I sipped it slowly and tried to look like I liked it. I couldn't get into drinking beer. I went over the kitchen and started to look at the bottles. Vodka, Gin, Rum, Whiskey and peach schnapps. I opened the schnapps and smelled it. Wow! It smelled so good, not like the nasty whiskey. I poured myself a glass of Coke and mixed some schnapps in there. I mixed it up and took a big gulp. Wow! This is the way to go, I thought.

At first I didn't say much. I just sat around and watched everyone interact like I was watching one of my movies. Then, as the everyone started to get drunk and stoned, they started to actually talk to me. I wasn't expecting that. Mackenzie was talking to me about how health class was so stupid. I said "I know." I didn't know what else to say.

"Mr. Hollister is such an idiot, huh?" my next line that came out.

"Ugggh, he's constantly yelling at me about my skirt and makeup. I hate him."

"Yea, fuck him."

I had sat behind Mackenzie since the beginning of the year, and she never said one word to me. Now, it was like we were friends! It was like I got the cool pass from Martin and it was ok for people to talk to me now. I don't get it. Well, I do get it but it's not right.

The night started to get blurry after a few Cokes and schnapps. At some point Darcy and Cecilia showed up, I don't know when. I was already drunk by then. I didn't even see them come in, I heard Darcy laugh and looked over to see her in the kitchen pouring a drink. She was talking to some people, so I left her alone for the time being.

I kept close to Martin most of the night until he disappeared with Alissa. I assume they went to have sex. Then I glommed onto Darcy and Cecilia.

I have to admit, it was strange seeing Darcy outside of school. She was looking really good in her funky outfit and was constantly smoking which made her look like a bad ass.

Darcy and Cecilia were both pretty drunk, but were acting normal because they were used to drinking. I was getting drunk and didn't' realize what would happen if I kept drinking. I,ve only been drunk a few times and it never ended well.

I don't know when it happened, but the drinks caught up with me. I lost all ability to function like a normal person, and was so wasted that I was jumping on the couch and making fun of everyone. All the thoughts that I kept in my brain over the past two years were coming out. I was a completely different person, I wasn't scared of anything!

I called them all out on their bullshit. I told them they were all "fake" and their whole image of being the druggies was non-sense.

"Down at the bottom, we can see it all!" I remember saying. I was pointing all around the room when I was ranting, and they all laughed like I was a crazy person.

"We have plenty of time to judge you for who you really are," I said drunk as hell.

In grade school, I was friends with a bunch of the people in the room, and when they got to high school, they completely changed and assimilated with the pot heads. Even though I was blasting them, they continued laughing. They were probably laughing at me but who cares. I felt like the life of the party.

By the end of the night I don't remember much, just that the room was spinning and I was seeing double. I felt nauseated, so I went out to the balcony and puked my brains out. Luckily it didn't hit any cars below, just the street. It was all chunky from the pizza we ate. I felt so much better after that. I remember Darcy taking me to the bathroom and then putting me in bed.

I woke up the next day still kind of drunk and queasy. My first hangover! I heard people talk about them before, and they're just as they described. Horrible! I walked around and the place was a mess. There were bodies on the floor, strewn about. I went to the toilet and puked again. It hit the spot. Puking is like hitting the reset button on a Nintendo when you're having a bad game; you just start over and begin again! When the rest of the people woke up, we sat around and drank coffee and made breakfast. They filled me in on what happened. It was embarrassing hearing how drunk I got. I didn't know I could get that crazy. The rest of the day we cleaned the place up and then drove home.

So at school on Monday, the whole class was talking about me. I heard from different people:

"Wow, I wish I was at that party, I heard you were nuts."

"Did you really puke off a balcony?"

"Dude, you gotta come to my next party and fuck shit up!"

"How much did you drink?"

It was a strange feeling. Nobody talked about me. Ever. And now, for a day, I was on everyone's minds. I didn't like it, to be honest. I hate attention, it has never suited me. Walking through the halls, I had to look down, because when I looked around, I assumed people were talking about me.

At lunch, Darcy told the table the whole story and everything that happened. There was a ton of exaggeration, but most of her account sounded like the actual night.

Surprisingly, it only lasted a day. On Tuesday, I didn't hear anything from anybody and I was at ease again.

THAT WAS ONE HELL OF A PARTY!!

January 24, 1997

It's getting so cold out! The high today was only 12 degrees. I only went out and kicked for 10 minutes against the shed and then said "screw it." I went in our nice warm house and played some PlayStation. It was a football game, so at least I was learning something, right? I don't know how much longer I can take it. Maybe I can set something up in our basement until the spring hits, so I can keep practicing kicking indoors.

January 31, 1997

This is hard to talk about. My grandfather died a week ago. I wanted to talk about this sooner but every time I sat at the computer, I couldn't bring myself to type. Since he's buried now, I feel it's ok.

It came out of nowhere. I was sitting around watching *The Simpsons,* and the phone rang, and my dad answered. He listened for about five seconds and then ran to talk to my mom. Then they said something happened to pop-pop, and they left.

I never really knew who my grandfather was. As a kid, my parents would drop me off at their house and my mom-mom, my, would take care of our every need. She let us watch whatever we wanted, and I loved how she made us personal pan pizzas for lunch; we never had them at home. My pop-pop would just sit in the back den and smoke cigarettes and watch TV. He loved *Married with Children* and *National Geographic Wildlife* videos. My brother and I would go back to the closet in the den to get puzzles and games and then go back to the other side of the house to play them. Sometimes, we would stay in there for a bit but never too long.

They had a super big lawn that we ranaround in and there was a creek in the woods out back. My pop-pop would take us back there, and we would catch frogs and sometimes find arrowheads. Sometimes he would find a box turtle while he was mowing and then give it to us as a pet. I loved going over there as a kid.

As I got older, I started to learn more about him. He was a sharpshooter in World War II and when he came back, he threw all his medals in the trash. I thought that was strange; I would have liked to have seen them. He should have been proud of his bravery. I asked my dad about that and he said he had bad memories of the war and didn't want to remember anything. I guess I can understand that.

My parents sat us down and told us what happened with my grandfather two days after it happened. He killed himself. With a shotgun. I found out that last part from my sister. My parents said he was depressed for a long time, and he wanted to die. That was how Hemingway did himself. I learned that in English class. My mom said he used to talk about it when the kids weren't around, so it wasn't totally out of the blue. It was sad; he had a whole family who loved him, but that didn't matter; he was sick.

The funeral was weird, it was the first time I had seen a dead body. Nobody else had died in my family so I had been pretty lucky. He just looked like a wax dummy. I wondered how they had an open casket if he had shot himself. He must have shot himself in the chest and they funeral people covered it up. There wasn't much crying either. My aunt on my dad's side of the family kind of lost it for a while, but I think everybody else knew he was happier. He was 72 when he died, so I think that's pretty old. It seems really old to me. I think death is less somber the older you get.

While I was sitting there, I thought about all my other grandparents. I started to think about when they die, I'm going to have to do this again. Life can be so depressing sometimes. I hope when I die that they have a big party for me and people drink and laugh and talk about the good times.

I hope that wherever he is, it is nice and he is happy now. I don't know what my grandmother will do. She can't drive a car and has been with him her whole life. That's what makes me really sad. He used to drive her to the grocery store in his blue 80's station wagon and would wait in the car while she went shopping. I thought that was odd but it worked for them.

February 4, 1997

I heard in theology class on Monday that my cousin, Stacy, is dating Eric Holbrook. She's the same age as I am and we have been going to school together since kindergarten. She was always pretty and talented all those years growing up together. She's a natural artist and can draw beautiful pictures and she also gets straight A's. When you are in the same grade in the same school as a cousin, you're secretly competing with them. It wasn't really any competition though. She blew me away on all fronts: grades, looks, popularity, and talent. I really didn't have any of that. I was a good athlete, but when it came to showing up on game day, I usually lost all confidence and shit the bed.

It was always weird with us; we should have been good friends, but I guess I was intimidated by her beauty and popularity. We would say "hi" to each other when I was over at my aunt's house but that was it. She has a younger brother, Mark, who I have more in common with. From 3rd to 8th grade, I would sleep over at their house with my younger brother Don and we would play Sega Genesis all night long.

Sometimes Stacy would have a sleepover at the same time and invite a few of the other pretty girls from my grade. They would mostly stay in Stacy's room all night. Once in a while one of them would go to the kitchen, and I got to see them in their pajamas. My grade school crush, Laura Mitchell, was her best friend. She would be over there all the time, and it killed me that I could never talk to her. She would be a few feet away on the couch and I just locked up and said nothing.

The closest time I came to hanging out with Stacey was after 8th grade graduation. She had a huge pool party and invited all the cool kids. I got an invitation in the mail with a list of the kids that were invited. My name didn't look right on there. I assumed that my aunt forced her to invite me; there was no way she wanted me there. I had never been to a party so I just wanted to stay home. My mom made me go and it was a strange experience.

When I showed up, a few of the guys on the basketball team were shooting around and did a double take when they saw me. Then, they shook my hand and said "I didn't know you were coming!" and then passed me the ball. The rest of the party was like that; all the cool kids I never talked to completely accepted me for the day. I said a quick "hi" to Stacy and that was our only contact for the party.

Now that Stacy is in high school, our relationship is still based on avoidance. She's in all honors classes and I am in all Group 3 classes, which are all the dumb kids, so we never share any classes but I pass her in the hallway and see her at lunch. It's weird, because we both act like we don't know each other. I don't know why. I'm a shy person, but I should be able to acknowledge my cousin with a simple "hi," but I can't. She's one of the popular elite, and I'm just some dork. I'm pretty sure most people in school don't even know we're related. Isn't that crazy?

As I was walking to lunch today, I saw Stacy and Eric talking at her locker. He had his hand above her head and his face right near hers. He has thick arms and a pug like face. I wonder what she sees in him. He seems like a lunk head. I think Eric Holbrook is already her 3rd boyfriend this year.

I think Stacy's going to go onto to big things after high school. How can she not? She has looks, brains and is creative. I'm so jealous of her because I don't have any of those. I'm just a lazy frump destined for nothing.

February 7, 1997

The disciplinarian Mr. Girard caught stoner Jack Cleasock and Penelope Alverez, the exchange student, smoking pot in his car in the parking lot on Thursday. He had them in his office pretty much all morning until his parents and Penelope's guardians showed up. I heard a rumor that she might get kicked out of school and have to go back to Spain. Jack already got suspended for a week. It was all the buzz around school the last two days.

All the girls are happy that she might get kicked

out. Penelope kind of made it that way though. She came into school acting all hot and shit, and I've found out that girls don't like that. They act all catty and turn on each other. I see the football players act like that, but it's not the same. Guys compete with each other for chicks, but they can still be friends. I don't think Penelope is friends with even one girl. I've only seen her talking to guys the whole time she was here.

I hope she doesn't get kicked out. She serves as a reminder to Darcy that Matt is a god damn cheater. If she leaves, then maybe they'll get back together. Darcy still talks about Matt and about how much she loved him and that maybe she made a mistake in breaking up with him. When I hear her talk that way I want to pull out my hair. Cecilia tries to talk some sense into her but I don't think she listens to anybody. How can she think like that? I guess girls are attracted to guys who seem larger than life. That's motivating me to keep kicking. I'm nowhere close to where I want to be, but it's getting easier.

February 9, 1997

It's strange going over to my mom-mom's house now. She's all alone there. She seems fine, but I don't know. They were married for a really long time. I wonder what it's like to lose your life partner like that. I couldn't imagine. I can't even imagine having a girlfriend, so that thought is way above my head. In the end, we all die alone, I think. We like to have this nice picture of our family around you saying goodbye as we pass, but it rarely happens. I'm sure I am going to die alone and I I'm ok with that.

I haven't been in the back TV room yet. I see the door closed from the kitchen, and that's as far as I go. I don't know if I ever want to go back there again. The front of the house is just fine from now on.

Even the garage is creepy. My grandfather had a ton of tools and every one of them had his initials *L.W.* The blue station wagon is useless now, since my mom-mom can't drive. The car is actually really nice and kept up; that was one thing he cared about. I guess they will end up selling it.

I hope she's ok, I really do.

February 10, 1997

So Penelope is gone. Apparently, she violated some rule they had about foreign exchange students. I heard that it wasn't even the pot, it was because it was on school grounds. That was where she fucked up. I don't know; that might be true; it might not be. I heard so many different things; I don't know what to believe.

Her guardians were cleaning out her locker today with Mr. Girard watching. All three of them looked really pissed.

"That girl, she is a hell cat, it's not your fault," Mr. Girard said to them as they gathered her belongings.

By the end of the day, someone had taken her

locker and put their stuff in there.

Bunch of savages in this school.

February 15, 1997

On Friday, at lunch, the greatest thing ever happened to me…I got invited to another party! And even better, it's at Darcy's house! She said her mom was going to New York to visit her dad who was working in the city. I had never been to Darcy's house, I only heard of how nice it was so I was curious to see what it is like. She was adamant that it wasn't a party, but more of a get together. It didn't matter to me, I was just happy being invited to a girl's house. I told her I would have to bring Ralph and Ronnie because I didn't have any other way of getting there. It was frustrating, because people in my grade were turning 16 and were getting their licenses, and I had to wait until March.

I didn't even know who was going to be there, that was the strangest part. I only knew Darcy from the lunch table. She had a whole other life outside of school that I only heard about. Part of me didn't want to go, because I would stick out like a sore thumb. I wanted Jerry to go but she said that he would tell too many people about it, and then it would turn into a huge party. She said her parents had expensive things all around the house, and she didn't want anything to break.

At first, Ronnie didn't even want to go to the party. He hated them, because he didn't drink or smoke pot. He said he tried going to a few football parties, but it wasn't for him. His dad was an alcoholic bartender, and I think it really messed with his head. I can understand why he wants to stay clean. Luckily, I never had to deal with that; my home is stable compared to his.

I've known Ronnie for about three years now and every year he's living somewhere else. His parents divorced when he was young, and he just moves around with his dad now. His brother and sister live with his mom. He likes living with his dad, because he can do whatever he wants. It's kind of amazing because he could be a major fuck up, doing drugs and skipping school, but he continues to stay on the straight and narrow path.

After an hour of me and Ralph badgering him in his parents basement, he finally caved. "Fuck it, let's go. You got two hours and then I'm leaving." Ralph jumped up and ran out telling his mom he was going out. "Where you go?" she yelled in broken English. "Out!" he shouted back.

I was jealous he could get away with stuff like that. My parents always gave me the run around, asking me every detail when I was going out. He could curse in his house and his mom didn't seem to care. It had to be because of the language barrier. Like if I hear an Italian curse word, it means nothing to me. It must be like that when she hears "Fuck."

We loaded up in Ronnie's white Neon and were there in 10 minutes. She lived in one of those developments that were hidden in plain view, and all the houses were enormous. There wasn't a gate but there could have been. As we were driving through, Ralph said the houses looked nice, but were built like cardboard. "Fucking McMansions," he said. I started to laugh. "Make sure you park far away, Darcy said she didn't want it to look like she was having a party." Ronnie groaned and then complied, he was hating every minute of this.

We walked up to the door and rang the bell. I heard a dog start to bark, and then my whole body was stiff with nerves. I wished we had smoked pot or something before we went. I never had any though. I actually never even bought pot; if I do smoke it gets passed to me in a car or in the back alley.

Darcy answered the door with a big smile on her face, and she was holding a cup. "Hey Nic! I can't believe you made it," she said. She gave me a big hug, and her breasts were right on against my body. Her hair smelled like smoke and Jolly Ranchers, it was wonderful. Behind her, some guy I had never seen before was holding her giant German Shepard back. I could hear rock music blaring from the basement.

"Come on in," she said. I could tell she was already a little wasted. She seemed happier than normal. We walked to the kitchen where there were a few bottles of liquor and some soda.

"Beer is in the fridge or you can mix something," she said. "Come outside then, we're all smoking."

Outside on her deck was a cloud of smoke and people all hanging out in the cold January air. I got a beer from the fridge for Ralph and me each and Ronnie had a Coke.

We stood out there and Darcy offered me a smoke. I turned her down, which when I think about now was dumb. I should really start smoking, it seems like you're immediately cooler when you smoke. It's like being a part of a club.

It was awkward at first being out there with a bunch of people I never talked to. At least Cecilia and Martin were there; they were really the only ones I knew. I talked to her for a while, which was nice. I liked how she wasn't smoking like the rest of them. "Ugggh, gross," I remember her saying. She even had makeup on and looked kind of pretty.

The rest were people I passed in the halls or sat in class with. I knew their name, they might have known mine but there was never any interaction. They were mostly low level stoners and a few field hockey girls. There were also a few public school guys there; they looked shady as usual. Maybe 15 people tops were there. 18 with Ronnie, Ralph, and me.

Everyone started to get cold, so we went back inside and then down to the basement. It was a huge full finished basement with pool and a bar and even a jukebox. It was really neat. There was a huge glass bong on the bar and the whole place stank of weed.

When we got in the basement, Ralph and I were still nervous, so we starting chugging beer to make ourselves feel better. Ronnie looked at us like we were idiots, and he was kind of right. Then things started to get better. Ralph started going around talking to everyone; he wasn't shy like I was. He started to make the girls laugh with his drunken antics. He even started to dance with Cecilia and was twirling her around.

The bong started going around, and the CD player was playing alternative music like Garbage and Sound Garden. I took one hit off the bong, and then I was out of it the rest of the night. I don't remember much after that. The only thing I recall is walking around looking for Darcy.

I walked whole first floor of the house looking for her. In the process, I looked at all her family pictures. She was a really cute kid, and the family looked so clean and perfect in those pictures. In reality, they were really screwed up. That is the American way, I thought. As long as you make a lot of money and have a nice house, it doesn't matter if your kids are screw ups. Sweep it all under the carpet with your money. What a joke.

I saw Cecilia in kitchen and asked, "What happened to Darcy?"

"Oh, she disappeared with one of those public school guys."

"Oh, seems about right." I wasn't surprised; she barely talked to me all night long.

"Yea, she's ridiculous. She took the Matt thing pretty hard and has been acting out ever since."

At that point, I just wanted to go home. It was pointless, Darcy was never going to look at me as boyfriend material unless I made the football team, or started getting her weed. Even then, I think she wouldn't care.

Ronnie dropped us off in the back alley and I crashed on Ralph's basement couch. His mom was in bed and his dad was a night janitor for North Park High, so the coast was clear.

I would never come home drunk to my house. I know my mom would wake up and see it on my face. It's just easier sleeping over at Ralph's. Besides, his mom made me coffee and breakfast in the morning, which was amazing.

March 1, 1997

Computer class is kind of a joke. Freshman year, we had typing class which was actually the only class in which I learned something. It was excruciating trying to adjust my fingers to the keyboard and not look at the keys. It took a good two months to get up to 50 words a minute. It was an integrated class so some of the honors students were in with us. They were at 90-100 words a minute by the end of the semester. It was a pretty cool skill to have, though; I was glad they taught us that.

This year, they're trying to show us how to use Microsoft Word and Excel. I had been using these programs for a few years so it's a pointless class for me.

Our teacher, Mrs. Cirta is really short and really annoying. She seems like a nice person but she takes the class too seriously. I heard about something called "Napoleon Syndrome" where short people have to act all bossy to make up for their stature. I wonder if that's a real thing? If so, Mrs. Cirta definitely has it.

Like, for instance, when she gives us a class assignment, and then we finish early, why can't we play solitaire? She walks around the room every 10 minutes and makes sure nobody is screwing around.

Recently, my friend Gary found a way to play old Nintendo games on the computer. He said it's called "emulation." I don't even know how it works, but he was playing *The Legend of Zelda* on his computer the other day. It was sick! He gave me the files and I put them on my computer.

So my move is when Mrs. Cirta is sitting at her desk in the front of the room, I fire up one of my favorite games, *Mike Tyson's Punch-out!!* on my computer. Then, when she walks around, I shut the window and act like I'm working.

It's starting to catch on. Some other kids are seeing us play and have been asking how we're doing it. Eventually our secret will be out there and it will only take one idiot to get caught and ruin our fun. I actually look forward to class, reliving my childhood is freaking sweet!

March 4, 1997

I feel so bad about myself lately. I haven't kicked a football since January. It's just been so damn cold. February was brutal! It sucks because I was getting really good, but I couldn't keep hitting that hard rock anymore. I was getting sick all the time being out in the cold. I know it's just an excuse, but I got sad after my grandfather died. I have always been lazy, and those two things combined made me not want to do anything.

It's starting to warm up, though. I saw the weather forecast, and by the end of the week it is supposed to be in the 50's. I will be ready. A month off isn't that bad, I can get back into the groove of things rather quickly.

Oh yea, something gross happened at McDonald's the other day. In March they bring out the Shamrock Shake, which is a green milk shake that's mint flavored. It's a dumb gimmick McDonald's only sells around St. Patrick's Day. I was working the front cash register and the really fat assistant manager woman was drinking a shake and yelling about how it tasted like cum.

She was going around and having some of the girls in the kitchen test it out to see what they thought. It was so disgusting. Then, she came over to me and I asked what I thought. "How would I know?" I said in defense. Luckily there were no customers around at the time to see what was going on. Late at night before closing is when people start to act up.

I don't like her very much. She usually smells like body odor, has a thin dark mustache, and constantly talks about how her kids are all drug addicts. She was loud too. I don't like loud, boisterous people. Most of the time she just sits in her office like Jabba the Hut, eating chicken nuggets and doing crossword puzzles. Her pregnant daughter came in one time and looked terrible; worse than her. I saw her light a cigarette when she left, which seems insane. I wanted to call the police for child abuse.

I've got to get a new job. I don't want to be around those people anymore. Just the initial smell of disgusting greasy fast food when I clock into work makes me nauseated.

March 10, 1997

So it finally happened. Darcy got back together with Matt. I heard the rumor in 2nd period Marketing and by lunch, I heard it from the horse's mouth. When Darcy told me, it was like the words were coming out in slow motion. She seemed so happy too, like she was in love again. I'm still in shock.

The story goes that over the weekend, Darcy and Matt were at the same party and were avoiding each other all night long. As the night went on and, as they both got drunker and drunker, they started to talk and then the talking went to kissing. The kissing went to, well, you know. I don't even want to picture it.

I'm so pissed that Penelope got deported back to Spain. Her leaving was like wiping the slate clean; it was like Matt never cheated. I wish I could smack some sense into Darcy and ask her why she's doing this. Clearly this guy is an asshole, and she saw it when he cheated, but again he tricked her. I can't even imagine being able to get a girl to go out with me in the first place and this guy gets a girl he cheated on to go back out with him! That is some real sorcery.

This just reinforces what I'm doing. Enough with this other non-sense of video games and movies, the football team is my destiny now. Nothing will stop me. Ok, I'm not giving up movies, but the video games are a waste of time and will get me nowhere in the end.

What I realized with video games is that I don't even like playing them that much. I got hooked as a kid back in the 80's when I would go over my neighbor's house. He had a Commodore 64, and I would go over there and watch him and his older brother play. I had never seen anything like it. They would ask me to play and then I would just hit the button and then die real quick. For me, it was more a social thing. I was around other kids watching them play.

It doesn't matter now; I'm taking a long break from video games, hopefully forever.

March 13, 1997

I went out after school to the baseball field for two hours today. It was all nasty and muddy from the ground melting. I didn't care though. I was so pissed off about Darcy that I just kicked and kicked. Most of them were not even close, because the ball was wet and covered in mud. It got rid of all of my anger though. You should have seen my sweatpants and cleats when I was done; they were totally covered in mud. My dad looked at me and laughed when I got home. I still didn't tell him that I was going to try out for football. I didn't want to raise any expectations. I'll continue to claim this is just my hobby.

I didn't even play video games when I got home! I was so proud of myself. I did a little homework, watched some TV, and went to bed.

March 17, 1997

I usually hate my birthday but this one is special.
FINALLY 16 YEARS OLD!!!! It's been so hard watching
all my friends get their driver's licenses and buy cars and
drive to school or go wherever they want. I want – no - I
need that kind of freedom. For too long I've sat on that
damn bus and ridden around for an hour to get home.
It's taken so much life out of me. It ends soon, that's for
sure.

Since my birthday is on a Monday this year, we
had a party on Saturday. I'm ready for these parties to
end; it feels like I'm too old for them. My mom insisted
though. The gifts and money part of the birthday are
cool but I hate the attention. I don't do well being
praised and seeing people happy for me. I'm not used to
it. It's easier for me to stay in the background and stay
unnoticed. I do like that people have to be nice to you
all day, no matter what. That is pretty sweet. But then,
the next day, everything goes back to normal, and you're
treated exactly the same as you were the day before your
birthday. It's too much of a tease.

The party consisted of just my family: aunts,
uncles, cousins, and grandparents. Friends were never
invited for the family parties. If I wanted a party for
them, then it would be separate. I don't know why this
is; it has been that way forever. I felt bad seeing my
cousin Stacy at my party. It was Saturday night, and I
could tell she had plans. She was on our phone quite a
bit talking to people.

Right after we had cake, a car pulled into our

driveway, and she ran out the door. It must have been her boyfriend or some of her friends. I wondered where they were going. At least she got to leave, and I didn't ruin her whole night with my stupid party. This is the last one, ever. I don't care how much money I get from these things. I'm done.

Every year since I can remember, people give me some kind of birthday card about St. Patrick's Day. I don't know why it's such a big deal. We don't even get the day off for school, what kind of crackpot holiday is this?

Only a few people at school today even knew it was my birthday. I'm too shy to say anything. Some people actively walk around on their birthday like you should worship them or something. It seems like they just want any kind of attention possible. They should at least give you off the time from school on your birthday. That would make the most sense.

Most of my presents sucked. But I did get a Sony Disc-Man from my parents and my sister got me two CDs: Greenday's *Dookie* and Nirvana's *Nevermind*. Finally no more tapes!

When everyone left I went up to my room and listened to both CD's all night long. It was glorious. I loved laying on my bed all alone and listening to music. Nobody bothered me and the world was just right.

March 19, 1997

It's brutal now that Darcy is back together with Matt. It's like she's was a different person when she's with him. When she was single, she was her own person; a really cool chick. And now, she's under that Matt spell again. At lunch, she starts talking about the baseball season coming up and going to some games. Nobody at the table wants to hear it; even Cecilia rolls her eyes.

I get it in a way. He's a senior and the starting varsity short stop who can hit home runs. That's pretty cool. It would be like me dating the head cheerleader. I would do whatever she said whenever she said and would lose all identity.

I watched an episode of *Seinfeld* the other day, and Jerry was saying to Elaine that breaking up is like tipping over a Coke machine; it doesn't happen on the first push. You have to tip it back and forth a few times before it smashes to the ground. Maybe that's what's going on. She wants one more steamy go around with the high school hunk. Whatever, I can't do anything about it except keep building myself up.

I'm biding my time right now. The kicking is going really well because I'm back to it every day. Matt will graduate soon and hopefully I'll be on the football team next year. It'll be like a perfect storm; she'll have to notice me then.

March 21, 1997

I went to get my drivers permit the day after my birthday and passed with flying colors. It was a dumb test with pointless questions that most drivers wouldn't be able to answer. One of questions was:
You may make a left turn at a red light if you are turning from
A)   the right lane of a one way street onto a two way street
B)   the left lane of a one way street onto a two way street
C)   the right lane of a one way street onto another one way street
D)   the left lane of a one way street onto another one way street
This was one of the example questions on the pretest in the booklet, so I showed it to my dad. I asked him to answer the question, and he didn't even think it was legal to turn left on a red light. I told him the answer was "D" and he goes, "Huh, never knew that. "

March 24, 1997

When I got to school this morning, I heard that Robert Plant and Jimmy Page are going to be touring this summer! Robert Plant was the lead singer of 70's band Led Zeppelin, and Jimmy Page was the guitarist. Ralph said he heard on the radio that they're going to be playing all the Led Zeppelin hits! He said his brother

Vince and his friends were planning on going.

"I mean, we can probably tag along; the tickets go on sale Friday. You can only get two per person, so I'll go with him and get you a ticket."

"Yea, we have to go to this, who knows if they'll ever do this again?"

"I know, you're right. They are 50 bucks but fuck it."

As it turned out, there were people talking about the concert all day. I know most of the kids don't listen to Led Zeppelin or know all the songs or the lyrics or which band member used which symbol. They just want to go to a concert and drink and look cool. The popular kids mostly listen to rap and pop; they are so lame. Yet, they are the ones who are accepted and I'm the outcast. At least Darcy likes old music.

I love Led Zeppelin. I never knew about them until I started hanging out with Ralph. His brother was a super fan and was always playing their music in his basement. They had such a great 70's sound. He got me hooked right away. He let me borrow some concert picture books about the band and I thought they were so bad-ass. You had Robert Plant, the lead singer, Jimmy Page on guitar, John Paul Jones on bass and John Bonham on drums. They were like a metal version of The Beatles. It sucks that John Bonham died in 1980, which led to the breakup of the band. The book said he died when he drank 40 shots of vodka one night. What a maniac!

At lunch that day we talked about who was the best singer ever. Of course I said Robert Plant; Darcy loved Jim Morrison, Gary said Freddy Mercury, Ralph said Roger Daltry, and Bill said Kurt Cobain. We had a lot of those stupid conversations. Last week we talked about the show *Friends,* and who was the hottest chick on the show. We all concluded that Phoebe was the worst, but it was split between Monica and Rachel. I was always a Monica man.

The week before, we debated who would win in a fight, a bear or a lion. The consensus was the bear because it had thicker skin. I love random arguments like that.

March 30, 1997

Easter, what a brutal holiday. As you get older, the holidays that used to be fun are now excruciating. I wouldn't mind so much if it wasn't for church. These "part-time Catholics" as my mom calls them only show up on Christmas and Easter. That means the whole place is jammed up, and we have to get there a half-hour early to get a seat, or we have to stand the whole time.

Easter mass is the longest as well. It can go almost an hour and a half sometimes if the priest gets chatty during his homily. So, arriving the half hour early and considering travel time, it's over two hours!

It's pointless for me to go; I never pay attention and don't sing any songs. I usually just look around and see if there are any girls from Lindsburg Catholic there.

If I do see a pretty one, I focus on her the whole time and think about how I could possibly ask her out. I know it'll never happen but it gets me through the mass.

Later we went over to my other mom-mom's house, my mom's mother. They're pretty much opposite in a lot of ways to my dad's parents. They are strict Catholics and have a healthy normal relationship. It's kind of amazing how happy they look. My other pop-pop "Charlie" doesn't sit around and smoke and watch TV. He's always smiling and looks full of life. He even has a huge garden in the back yard that he loves to be in all day. I don't know if he was in the war or not, I'll have to ask my mom. I've never heard them talk about it, so maybe not. That could be why they're so different.

On Easter my mom's sister and her kids come over, and we have an egg hunt in the yard. It has been a tradition in the family since I was a baby and it was something I looked forward to as a kid. Now I'm getting older, it's getting lame. My cousin Stacy and I looked at each other like *we are way too old for this stupid shit*. We ended up picking up eggs because one of them had some money in it. We did it slow though;, to make it look like we didn't care. It is hard being in between a child and adult. They didn't know what to do with us, and we didn't know either.

April 5, 1997

I failed my driver's test. What the fuck! This is

the worst day ever! I was so pumped to take out my El Camino this weekend and then be able to drive to school. God, I can't take much more of the bus.

Here is what happened. I went with my sister's new boyfriend to the DMV. His name is Roy and he is a really nice guy. He is another huge dude but not a body builder like the last one, he looks like a football player. He is the nicest one yet. When I told him about my driving test on Easter, he offered me his nice small 1991 Ford Taurus, which is so much easier to drive than my loud, old El Camino. Parallel parking is my only weakness but with his car I would be fine.

So I get in the car with the driving test guy and he's outside the car with a clipboard and asks me to turn on the headlights, wipers, turn signals and even the heat and air conditioning. I'm feeling good at this point because it's all going smoothly. Then he asks me to "Hit the high beams."

"What?" I say.

"The high beams, turn them on," he says.

"I don't know what you mean," I say.

"Get out of the car," he says.

"What?" I say.

"Get out of the car," he says.

So I get out and he shows me the high beams and then said I failed. My dreams were dashed by this toupee wearing middle aged failure. I wanted to punch him in the face. I asked him if we could drive and he said no. Roy couldn't believe what an asshole he was.

"I should crush that guy's head like a pimple!" he yelled.

I was almost ready to cry but that made me feel

better. I hope Sarah stays with this guy; he seems like a cool dude.

So here sit, on another Friday night, with no car and no plans.

What pissed me off the most was when we were driving home, I looked in the cars passing by and they looked like morons. How did they have a license and I didn't? The problem was that the high beams on my El Camino were on the floor. That was how they made them back in the 60's and 70's. My dad never showed me where they were at or that they even existed. That is on him, I don't blame myself for that. At least in two weeks I can retest. Next time I'll be ready. Two more weeks of the bus...

April 6, 1997

I got my first double CD. It's called *Melancholy and the Infinite Sadness* by The Smashing Pumpkins. I heard a bunch of the songs on the radio before and I saw it in Circuit City and had to buy it. It was a toss-up between that and *Physical Graffiti* by Led Zeppelin. Ralph's brother let me borrow the Zeppelin I so I had already heard that a few times. I wanted something newer.

My favorite song on the album is called *Bullet with Butterfly Wings*. It's so angry and I can relate to it.

Billy Corgan, the lead singer of the group, is right; the world is a vampire. It sucks everything from you, and then you still have to keep going on, getting up every day and pretending to be happy. That's why I like it too; he doesn't put on a face.

He is a super famous rock star and he says:

Despite all my rage, I am still just a rat in a cage.

That is exactly how I feel on a daily basis. I'm trapped in this world and none of this was my choice. I go from home to the bus to school and then back to the bus and then home again. It's such a shit cycle. I suppress my anger and sadness the best I can, but it gets to be too much sometimes. If Billy Corgan can't be happy, how will I ever be? Hopefully when I get my license, things will get a little better.

April 10, 1997

I know I haven't said anything about kicking lately; it's mostly because I really didn't have any updates. I'm going out to the field a few days a week for about an hour, but couldn't get past 40 yards. As much as I try, my leg just can't kick it any farther, I was really frustrated. It was like when my dad would go on a diet, and he would lose 10 pounds really fast and then hit a "plateau" and not be able to lose any more. I was at the same place.

While I was walking around the sports section of Wal-Mart, I saw these things called "ankle weights." I had never seen anything like it. They are supposed to be used for when you run to increase leg strength. I had a different idea. It was hard spending 25 bucks on them, but I had to try something.

When I got home, I went up to my room and put one on my right leg. I started to do my kicking motion, over and over with the weight strapped to my leg. After a few times, I could feel the burning in my leg. I knew that was either good or bad. I kept at it for another half hour and then went out to the shed to kick some balls.

I lined up, and the first kick felt like nothing. I slammed that thing like never before. My leg felt so light. I realized it wasn't about strength, but about leg speed. It was when I played baseball and would warm up with a weight on the bat and then without it, the bat felt like a feather. I cracked the code!

April 23, 1997

Sometimes, life can be bearable. And this is one of those days.

I got my license yesterday. I won't go over the boring details, but it happened. I went to a different testing center and the guy was really nice and didn't ask me to put on my high beams. He only asked for my turn signals and headlights. Then, we went for a drive, and then I left with my license. Amazing!!

When I got home, I drove my El Camino over to

Ralph's house. His two older brothers came out to look at the car since they were big gear heads. I lifted the hood and showed them the sweet 350 cubic inch Chevy motor. They seemed impressed. Then I drove around for a half hour all around town and then back home.

The next morning, I woke up an hour later than I usually did. There was no more bus from here on out. I had the keys to a loud machine from another time, and a magic card to let me drive it. I started the blue beast up and rumbled down the street with my Nirvana CD blaring.

Since I was just a sophomore, I didn't have a parking spot. That was only for juniors and seniors. I had to park in the street, like a peasant. It still was better than nothing.

As I drove by the school, I saw all the kids filing off the school bus, like I did for almost two years. They looked different now, like cattle that were going to the slaughterhouse. They had no choice. Not me. I was free now, forever able to choose my own direction. I could keep driving past the school and go down to the donut shop that Ronnie liked. I could go to a diner or just simply keep driving to New Jersey if I wanted.

Well, I didn't do any of that. I just found a spot on the street and parked and went to school. But I could have done any of those things…if I wanted.

April 27, 1997

Now that I have my license I can go wherever I wanted. Where do I want to go? That's the question. Mostly I just go to the movie rental store. New movies don't really interest me. I love to catching up on old ones that came out when I was young or even before I was born. The 80's are my favorite era. You could tell a movie was made in the 1980's right away. The John Hughes movies are something special. He could really capture how ridiculous high school was.

I don't remember much from the 80's as far as pop culture. I wasn't allowed to watch much on MTV. I did like Alf, I know that. That was my favorite show back then.

My sister, Sarah, was allowed to watch MTV non-stop. The music video for *Rock the Cradle of Love* by Billy Idol will forever be burned into my brain. When it first came out, it was constantly on my TV. I would watch it from the other room, so my sister didn't see me. If you don't remember the video, it featured a bombshell blond dancing around in a bra and panties. I didn't completely understand what was going on at the time but I knew I liked it.

John Cusak was one of my favorite 80's actors. I had already seen a bunch of his movies, and they were all really good. I know I had seen a picture of him somewhere holding a stereo, but I didn't know what movie it was. So on Friday night, I got in my car and drove to West Coast Video to find it. Driving around in the warm spring night in my El Camino was the best. The Chevy 350 small block produced a really nice rumble. I would get looks wherever I went in that thing. It was a real unique car. I know girls didn't really like it, but I didn't care; they don't know much about cars.

I like going to West Coast Video better than Blockbuster. Blockbuster is too corporate, and they don't have the movies with full nudity. As a freshman, Ralph, Ronnie and I went to Blockbuster to find a soft-core porn movie, and then we got it back to Ronnie's to watch it, and they didn't show anything! We kept fast forwarding it and there was nothing. Not even a nipple! It was such a joke. It's like that dumb show *Silk Stalkings* on the USA network, the same thing. They advertise it as this steamy hot show, and they never show any nudity. It was cool in 8th grade, but not now.

West Coast is kind of grimy and not as well-lit, which gives it an 80's feel. They even had a back room with the real hard core stuff. It was behind a curtain. I never had the balls to go back there. Chuck and Jerry went back there though. I was too afraid to get caught, but not them. I think they know the owner because he goes to Romano's for beer.

West Coast had better categories too. They have a section strictly dedicated to the 80's, a section called "Warped" which was all weird movies and a section with the employee picks. The one cashier girl usually has some good ones in there. I want to tell her that she has good taste in movies but she is really hot and has green hair. I don't think I would be her type.

As I was walking around the store, the movie jumped out at me. *Say Anything*. There he was John, *motherfucking* Cusak, right on the cover, holding that boom box. I picked it up and drove out of there. I made sure to cruise around for a half hour, just to relish my new found freedom. I even stopped at Wendy's and got a bacon cheeseburger and a soda. I never went to McDonald's. I had eaten so much of their food, it didn't even appeal to me anymore.

So when I got home I ran up to my room and popped the tape in. Let me tell you, this is a brilliant film. It was a cross between *The Sure Thing* and *Better off Dead*. It was a little goofy but also a nice love story. I feel like that I'm going through the same thing he is in the movie. He wants to be a kick boxer and I want to be a field goal kicker. Both ridiculous dreams. He loves some girl way out of his league. Same. He is a weird loner. Right on the money.

I don't know who wrote that movie but it was awesome. I wonder if it's based on reality. I think most movies are; that's where these writers get their ideas.

Say Anything : 5/5 stars

May 2, 1997

Out of the blue, Ralph got a date for the Sophomore Prom. I'm so pissed. A hot girl he works with at the retirement home was badgering him about him not going to his prom, so she said she would go with him. He didn't even have to ask her! What dumb luck. Uggggh. Now I feel like I have to go since he's going. We had a pact that we would never go to any prom and he broke it. I can understand though. We only made it because we assumed that no one would go with us. If a hot girl asked me, what would I say, "no?" Hell no, I would betray Ralph in a second.

After I heard that I walked around the next few days looking at potential girls who I could ask. It's dire. Our grade has absolutely nothing for me to approach. I just want some "ok" looking girl in the middle who won't get me too much attention. The problem is that even the ok looking girls were taken by some of the guys who are sort of popular. The rest are ghouls who would ruin any chance I have at a social life. I don't mean to be mean, but some of these girls barely shower. You can smell them and see the hair above their lip. They must have bad homes or something. I don't know; it's just depressing that I have no options.

May 7, 1997

Miraculously, I found a girl to ask! Her name is Sabrina Walder, and she sits two seats down from me in my computer class. She's a Junior and kind of cute and I would never even think about asking her but here is the thing, she's the sister of my friend Jack Walder. She was there the whole time! I talked to him and asked him if it was ok. He said he didn't care and later that day before computer class started I said to her

"Hey, do you wanna go to the Sophmore Prom with me?" I was terrified. I could barely get out the words. Just looking at her, she was older, developed and somewhat popular. I sat there for a second, and then she said "Sure!" like it was nothing. I let out a huge sigh and said "Thanks." She knew what it was, a pity date.

When some people found out that I had asked her, they tried telling me that she was dirty, and I could probably hook up with her. The guys had a field day with Jack, they messed with him non-stop saying that I was going to bang her. It was ridiculous. I had no delusions that Sabrina wanted anything to do with me. I was pretty sure she even had a boyfriend, but that didn't stop my knucklehead friends from trying to put things in my head. I was going to take her to the prom, and then I was taking her home.

May 9, 1997

I saw the best movie tonight. I had to write about it while it's still fresh. It's called *Dazed and Confused*. I had never even heard of it. I knew there was a Led Zeppelin song called *Dazed and Confused*. Maybe that's where they got the title from. Anyway, I was sitting watching TV when my sister and her boyfriend came in with a VHS from Blockbuster. She is back from college for the summer and its super annoying. I'm so jealous that college kids get out in May. It's so unfair.

Anyway, Sarah and Roy said it was a cool movie and they wanted to watch it, so said ok.

The movie opened with the song *Sweet Emotion* by Aerosmith and I could tell just by that that it was going to be good. The song played over shot after shot of cool old 60's and 70's hot rods like Camaros, Chevelles

Mustangs and souped up trucks. It was right up my alley. I wish Lindsburg was like that. I would fit right in with my El Camino.

Man, the 70's looked so cool. The cars were all hot rods and everybody was drinking and smoking. They had pool halls with foosball. I know it's just a movie but when my dad talks about the 70's, it's very similar. Nobody really cared back then; if you got caught drinking, the cop would drive you home and you would get a 25 dollar fine. Nowadays, I hear about kids getting caught drinking underage and it's an automatic three month suspension of your license.

My favorite character in the movie is this guy named Wooderson, he's so cool. He drives this sweet 1970 Chevelle and doesn't give a shit about anything. He wasn't even in high school anymore, and he was still trying to get the high school chicks. Maybe I can do that instead of going to college. I wish I could drop out of school and just work. It seems like such a waste of time showing up every day and not learning anything. I don't know, nowadays I look around and it's a totally different time.

Another part of the movie that was genius was the two nerds and the red head driving around all night having philosophical conversations. It really reminded me of what Ralph, Ronnie, and I did every weekend. It's too bad we didn't have a cute girl in the car with us.

I wish I grew up in the 70's or any other time than now. Now sucks. The music was better, the girls seemed cooler, and there were better cars. I'm pretty sure I would be so much happier back then but who knows? I don't. All I know is I'm going to practice kicking every day until I'm on the team. That the only thing I can control, that's all I have left.

Dazed and Confused: 4/5 stars

May 17, 1997

The day of the prom, I picked up Sabrina in my El Camino. She looked at the car and didn't really understand what it was. I think she was embarrassed at first, and then shrugged it off and laughed "Let's go have fun!" She had such a bubbly personality, I was so jealous. I had been beaten down so much in school that I was always pessimistic. It did help that she was a good looking, almost full grown, woman. She looked so good in that tight green dress too. God, I wish she was my girlfriend, I thought.

In the days leading up to the prom, I found out she did have a boyfriend. Some kid from a public school. I was happy though, it took off the pressure. I didn't know what I was doing, so there was no way I was making any moves, nor did I want to.

On the drive over, I told her I had never been to any dances and didn't know what to expect. She told me to not worry and she would lead the way. It felt good to be honest. I was never the type to pull off acting cooler than I really was. I think girls liked that. At least, I hoped they did.

"Are we going to stop at your house for

pictures?" she asked as we were driving.

"Nah, my parents aren't home."

"Oh, cool."

My parents bugged me to bring her over, but I told them no. They were so pissed. I didn't care, she was doing me a favor, and there was no reason for me to bring her to the house. If she was my girlfriend, then fine, but not Sabrina. I told them I would get a picture at the prom. I didn't want the attention. Dressing up in a suit was enough.

Why would I tease my mother with hopes I could get a girl? That would be just mean. I keep expectations low.

When we got to the school, I parked, and I walked with her to the gym. She put her arm around mine and we walked very slowly, because she had heels on. It was the first time I had walked with a woman like that. It felt like we were in a wedding or something. I was really nervous.

The hallways were all dark, and there were streamers everywhere. The school was unrecognizable. We could hear the music from the gymnasium and see lights flashing. When we entered there were tables all around the sides and we found our table and sat down. I didn't know what to say to her, I was just looking around the room at all the kids in our grade and who they brought. Some of the girls looked really slutty in their short skirts. I was glad Sabrina had a long dress; she looked better.

Eventually, the music started to kick in, and people started to dance. I didn't know how to dance so I just stared at them for a while. The popular kids all looked like they knew what they were doing. I was jealous of how easy life was for them. Most of them didn't even have zits. It wasn't fair.

Sitting at the table, watching them dance, I knew why I didn't go to dances. I had no clue what to do or what to say. I was jealous of Cecilia; she was at home avoiding all the pressure of these things.

It was especially excruciating seeing Darcy look all hot in her tight dress, dancing with Matt. I was frozen at the table. I didn't know what to do. Sabrina looked bored, and I know she wanted to do something. Ralph was up and about with his girl, dancing away without a care. Finally, I just said screw it.

"Come on, you need to show me what to do!" I said grabbing Sabrina's hand.

She smiled and we went out to the dance floor and I did my best to dance. I was honest and told her I didn't go to dances. "I'm used to being under a car when these things are happening." I said nervously. She laughed which felt good.

I don't remember much after that. I was just moving my body like a seizure victim and spinning her every few minutes. It must have looked ridiculous. It was fun though; once we started, I couldn't stop. Even Jerry came by and high fived me. Then the music slowed down and I put my hands around her waist, and swayed around. It felt really good to dance with a hot girl. I was just looking down most of the time making sure that I didn't step on her feet. When we were dancing I saw a few guys putting their hands on their date's asses. What balls!

At the end we got our pictures taken, and as the

dance was dying off, I saw a few groups of kids talking about the after parties. I asked Ralph what he was doing after, and he said "No idea."

"Go over and ask Jerry if there are any parties." I said to Ralph. Jerry was in a crowd of football players and their dates. He looked really animated talking to them, like they were planning an exciting night.

"Nah, we don't belong with them. We would just screw up his night." Ralph said.

"Yea, they would wonder why we're there."

So I just drove Sabrina home after the prom and told her I was eternally grateful. She laughed and gave me a kiss on the cheek, my first one! I didn't feel like going home, so I cruised around town for about an hour by myself. It was nice listening to the radio in my suit. The song *Wonderful Night* by Eric Clapton came on the oldies station, and it made me want to cry. I wished I had a woman like Eric Clapton was singing about.

As I drove, I imagined what everyone from the dance was doing at that moment. Jerry was with Katie Polk, Darcy was with Matt and Ralph was maybe with his girl. They were all probably drinking and hooking up, like normal high school kids, I thought. I was never going to be one of them. That kind of made me sad, I like being different, but what they had was something special. They were really living. You're only young once and most of the time, I feel I'm wasting my youth.

May 18, 1997

The best part about the warm weather for me is fishing. Ralph and I love to go fishing. Now that I had my license it's super easy to go whenever we wanted. If it's a nice day, after school, we meet at his house and then drive around to a local pond and go bass fishing for an hour or two.

Ralph's older brother loves to go fishing as well. Sometimes Ralph would go night fishing on the Delaware River with Vince and some of his senior friends, and he would invite me. That was cool because they would bring beer and pot, and we would make a fire. We would cast our lines out as far as possible with homemade dough bait that was made of corn meal and vanilla extract. It was the perfect bait for big carp.

I had never been carp fishing before I met Ralph. It was pretty cool, because you would be sitting there with nothing happening, and then, all of the sudden your line would be bent in half. You had to grab it real fast and yank back to set the hook. The carp were really strong and fat, which made reeling them in a challenge. I lost the first few because I didn't know what I was doing. I didn't set the drag on the reel, and the carp snapped the line with no problem. You had to tire the fish out like when you see guys catching Marlin on TV.

Night fishing is rare though. Most of the time it is just Ralph and I fishing at a small farm pond down the street. It was our only option because it is within bike riding distance of his house. We would use lures and try to catch the big bass in there. We had nowhere else to go back then, so it was perfect for us. We got to get out of the house, and nobody bothered us. I was happy to not be at school or at home, two places I didn't like very much.

We didn't get to go much last summer because of the no license or car problem. This year there is nothing stopping us from going whenever and wherever we want. High school is all about staying busy. As bad as it is, I can entertain myself with this stuff and know that one day, I will be free. Oh, yes, that day will be here soon enough.

May 21, 1997

So I've been using the ankle weights for a month now, and it's been wonderful. I started just swinging my leg with a 10 pound weight in my room for a half hour a day. Then, that got to be too easy, so I added the other 10 pounds and was swinging 20 pounds. I did that for about two weeks to really get my legs in shape and then went out to the baseball field. I lined up a few short kicks and blasted them with a new power. Then I put one at 40 yards and launched the ball over with no problem. I lined up a 45 yarder and slammed barely over the backstop. I smiled and looked around. It was just me, as usual. Nobody was there to see what I had done except a rabbit in the distance. It was another lonely accomplishment.

It took seven months but I did it. I fucking did it! It still doesn't mean I can actually kick in a real football game, but it was a goal that I set out to achieve and I did it. That's some Sesame Street shit there.

The only problem now is when I looked at my legs in the long mirror in the bathroom; my right leg is bigger than my left leg. It looks so weird! I'm going to have to start working out my left leg now. Uggggh, more work!

May 22, 1997

The end of the year is approaching and I still had perfect attendance. This is dangerous territory. The problem is that I never get sick or have any other reason to miss class. Other kids skip school without their parents knowing or miss for sports reasons or fake being sick. I just come to school every day and put up with it. The problem with perfect attendance is that at the end of the year they give out awards for academic reasons, sports, and activities. They have all the perfect attendees stand up on the stage in the gymnasium in front of the whole school.

I watched this happen my freshman year, and I heard a bunch of comments in the crowd about how big of losers those kids were. I couldn't be one of those people.

So, today, I faked being sick. I woke up and told my mother I had a stomach ache and couldn't go to school.

Sick days were the best because both my parents

worked. I stayed in bed until I heard the front door close and the car drive away. I was free! I jumped out of bed and made myself a big bowl of Cocoa Puffs and turned on the TV. I went right to TBS and watched back to back episodes of *Gilligan's Island*. I think Mary Anne is so hot and hoped she and Gilligan get married. I hated Ginger; she is such a tease.

After a while I got bored and played Playstation for an hour. Yes, I went back to video games after Greg from lunch let me borrow a game called *Resident Evil*. I've been working on beating this game for a while. *Resident Evil* is this really cool 3-D horror survival game where you play as a guy and a girl soldier and fight zombies and other monsters. The graphics are amazing compared to Sega Genesis. I love to turn off the lights in my room and play all night long. It's great to be this big muscular guy who could defend himself. In real life I'm so far away from that. Even the prospect of working out and lifting weights seems daunting. I'm afraid people would look at me and make fun of me for trying.

Later, I watched a porn tape that I borrowed from Jerry. I watched those movies with such curiosity and excitement. Those women were so developed, and they would hypnotize me. Sex is such a foreign concept to me; I wonder if I will ever get to do it. I can't believe Darcy was doing stuff like this! I thought. After I was done, my body went calm and then, a wave of shame fell on top of me. I looked at myself and hated what I saw.

The rest of the day I just laid around and watched more TV. I couldn't leave the house, so I was limited on options. About a half hour before my Dad got home, I jumped back in bed and acted sick again. It was no

Ferris Bueller's Day Off, but it was better than going to school!

May 23, 1997

The next day at lunch, Darcy asked me why I didn't come to school yesterday. I told her I faked sick to get the day off and she laughed.

"That's the first time I've seen you miss a day!" she said.

"It was sweet, I just watched TV and laid around all day."

"Nice, that's what I will be doing all summer."

"Really?"

"Yea, going to be at the shore, I can't wait."

"Must be nice! Us assholes will be working," Ralph said.

"Whatever, I might get a job while I'm there," Darcy said defensively.

I shook my head knowing that wasn't going to happen. Darcy never worked a day in her life.

After lunch in English class, Mr. Leyland told the whole class he was disappointed in us. It was nearing the end of the school year so he was trying to get in as many rants as he could in before the long summer of loneliness. He told us we were the worst class he had seen in a long time.

"How do you young ladies and gentlemen expect to get into college? All I've seen is a bunch of cheaters and lazy students. The only one who I have seen give any effort is Ms. Reynold's," he said looking at her.

I sat there and thought about it. He was right; the class was a Group 3 English class full of degenerates and dummies. Nobody gave a shit. Half of the class got the answers from the kids the year before because he used the same tests every year. So it was easy to cheat if you cared that much. I looked around the room and nobody seemed to care about what he was saying. I even shrugged it off because I wasn't expecting to get into college. Who cared about English anyway? I learned absolutely nothing in his class; it was all boring grammar, which seemed pointless to me.

"Half of the first year college students don't make it. That's a fact. I see so many kids goof around that first year and then they fail out. The teachers in college don't care if you screw around. They won't be after you for your homework. There probably won't be any homework. They probably won't even take attendance."

Wow! I thought. College seems cool! No homework and you don't have to go to class. Sign me up!

I was going to miss having Mr. Leyland as a teacher. He's a badass, an eccentric, a guy who plays by his own rules. Like Bruce Willis. Even though I didn't learn anything about English, I was thoroughly entertained by his crazy demeanor and his infatuation with Lilly Reynolds. The rest of my teachers were boring. They were cardboard cutout people who didn't inspire anything. They did their jobs and went home and cashed their check.

Not Mr. Leyland, he was an original.

May 24, 1997

I'm so pissed. I don't get angry at movies that much but this piece of shit took the cake. For months, I was so excited to see the sequel to *Jurassic Park* called *Jurassic Park: The Lost World.* The trailers looked awesome. They showed the T-Rex running around a city. The first movie was one of my favorites as a kid. I was only in 6th grade when it came out, so it was really scary. I watched it again when I was older, and it didn't scare me as much, but I still thought it was amazing. Nothing like it had ever been made; the dinosaurs were so realistic.

Friday night, Ralph, Greg, Bill and I got to the theater a half hour before it started. We figured the late show at 10:00 would be better since there would be no kids and the lines would be shorter. We were wrong. The place was still insanely packed and we had to wait a good 45 minutes in line for tickets. By the time we got in it was 11:00. Luckily they had it playing in a bunch of theaters, so we got into the 11:15 show.

It turns out that it was a total waste of time and money. Let me tell you what a piece of shit this movie is.

First off, they didn't bring back the main characters from the first one. Big mistake. Jeff Goldblum couldn't carry this movie on his own. He was a side character in the first one, and he should have remained one. Secondly, they teamed him up with this really annoying black girl who is his daughter and conveniently stows away to get on the island. I hate when they shoehorn in a character like that. The whole time, this girl ran around like a brat and was constantly getting into sticky situations. Jeff Goldblum's character kept yelling at her, and she never listened and then got almost eaten by dinosaurs at least five times. By the end I wished she had gotten eaten. By the time the T-Rex went on a rampage in San Diego, I had lost interest.

The ending was lame too. They just decided to leave the island alone and let the dinosaurs live on it. Right, like that would ever happen. Someone could go there and try to capture the dinosaurs, or the flying ones could fly somewhere else. In reality they would just nuke the crap out of it, destroying everything.

Even the dinosaurs looking cooler and better than they did in the original movie couldn't save this thing. You need good characters, good dialogue, and a good story. I didn't like anybody in this movie; I was rooting for the dinosaurs, which are supposed to be the bad guys.

What a disappointing start to the summer movie season.

Jurassic Park: The Lost World: 1/5 stars

May 25, 1997

I still can't believe I can drive wherever I want. The feeling is surreal. I love going to Best Buy for CD's, but it's about a half hour away, which sucks because they have the best selection for the cheapest prices. Most people just go to the music store in the mall called The Wall, but I don't like that place. It's way too expensive, and malls are lame. Like everything else that people enjoy, I go the opposite direction. I don't know why I'm like this. I should be hanging out there because girls are there, but I don't. I don't know why, it just seems stupid.

Ralph and I went to Best Buy last night, and whenever I go there, I immediately go to the movie soundtrack section. I love soundtrack CD's the most, because you get a good selection of different bands. And greatest hits too. Even though it is cooler to have the individual albums, the greatest hits are a better deal. On second thought, it depends on the band. Like, for Pink Floyd, their whole albums were like one big art piece. The songs were put in a special order, and they flow together. So a Pink Floyd greatest hits CD would be stupid.

Looking through the soundtracks, I came upon my new favorite CD: The *Dazed and Confused* sountrack. It's glorious.   Here are the songs:

Rock and Roll Hoochie Koo by Rick Derringer
Slow Ride by Foghat
School's Out by Alice Cooper
Jim Dandy by Black Oak Arkansas
Tush by Dusty Hill
Love Hurts by Nazareth
Stranglehold by Ted Nugent
Cherry Bomb by The Runaways
Fox on the Run by The Sweet
Low Rider by War
Tuesday's Gone by Lynyrd Skynyrd
Highway Star by Deep Purple

Rock and Roll All Nite by KISS
Paranoid by Black Sabbath

What a line up! I'm kind of pissed though. How could they leave out *Sweet Emotion*? It must be something with money, Aerosmith probably wanted a huge cut of the CD sales. I'm just glad *Tuesday's Gone* and *Fox on the Run* are on there. When I got out to my El Camino, I popped this in the CD player, and we blared it all the way home. I already listened through it three times since yesterday!

Music is great if you don't want to think about your life. When you have a good song on, all that matters is the song. When I put my headphones on in my room with my Disc-Man, I can get lost in those songs; it's better than any drug or beer. I like the sad stuff too; it makes me feel less lonely. It's nice to know that these rock stars feel down and out too. I bet most of them were band nerds in high school and they worked really hard to get famous so they could show up their classmates. I think that's what motivates a lot of these rich guys, like Bill Gates. He is like the nerdiest guy ever, and he's a billionaire.

May 28, 1997

I can't do it anymore. Marshall is such a fucking dickhead. He asked me if I was ready for the soccer season, and I told him I quit. He was like "Wow, you are a pussy, what the hell." I said it wasn't worth my time, and he kept calling me a pussy. What a jerk off.

I'm going to quit McDonald's soon. I don't understand Marshall, whenever it's just me and him working, he talks to me like a normal person and then if there are other people around, he turns into this evil super villain. He starts dumping on me to make himself look better. And of course, I just take it, because, that is what I always do.

Ralph's older brother just got him a job delivering auto parts and said they need one more driver. I'm going to apply. He said it's the best job ever, they pay $7.25 an hour, and you get to drive around and listen to the radio. The boss is super laid back, and a ton of people from Lindsburg work there. Cool people; not dicks like Marshall. I'm going over there on Saturday to fill out an application.

May 31, 1997

They passed out the yearbooks today. It didn't really affect me since I didn't order one. I got one last year just to see what was in it. Looking through it, I got depressed seeing all these fun activities and sports that my classmates were enjoying. They were all smiling and having a good time. I literally went to not one extracurricular event freshman year. I could remember where I was for pretty much everything: during the Father Son/Mother Daughter Dance, I went fishing with Ralph; during the Homecoming football game I was driving around with Dana Tisdal in his Isuzu

Trooper, blasting music; during the Winter Ball I was at home, in my parents garage, working on my El Camino; during the Freshman Dance I was driving around all night with Ralph and Ronnie in his Neon.

I didn't even vote for the student council president. I simply didn't care about any of it. I just removed myself mentally when I was at school and physically when it wasn't mandatory to be there.

We were required to go to the plays they had. I didn't mind them too much. Nobody paid attention though; it was just an hour and a half for kids to fuck around in the audience.

The biggest reason I didn't get a year book was because I felt ridiculous going around to people that I didn't even talk to and asking them to write a message in my yearbook. It seemed like something for girls to do. Yet, the kids in my school loved it. It was less pressure not having a book to sign. Also, it felt cooler to say that you didn't order one, like I didn't even care about looking at my picture. That was kind of true; I hated seeing my dorky head in there. I hated having my picture taken, I looked so awkward.

Darcy brought her yearbook to lunch so I just looked through it there. I only found a picture with the junior varsity soccer team and of course the mandatory profile picture. Some people had 5 to 10 extra pictures in there because they were so active outside of school. I did find one that was taken in the cafeteria; it was a picture of these pretty freshman girls in a line for food and I was fuzzy in the background. So that doesn't even count.

Darcy asked me to sign her book, which sucked. I didn't know what to write.   I hated having to come up with some witty message. I looked around and she already had a ton of signatures. Most of the guys she had sign it put their phone numbers in there.   I really wanted to write a message that said "don't fuck too many guys this summer," but I think she would have gotten mad.   Instead I wrote this:

Darcy,

It was a fun year at the lunch table, you and Cecilia cracked us up so many times. Have a fun summer at the shore and I hope to see you at the concert in July!

Nic

Nice and simple and easy. I wanted to leave my phone number but I chickened out. No wonder she doesn't look at me like a real man.

June 3, 1997

So I got the delivery job! I went in and filled out an application, and he interviewed me right there.   He only asked me a few questions mostly about when I could work. Then he said "When can you start?" He's such a cool laid back guy. It did help that Ralph and Vince said I'm a good worker.

As soon as he told me I had the job, I went over to McDonald's and quit. I gave them two weeks' notice, but they said I can leave whenever. So I told them I'll finish out the week and be done. I'll miss seeing the hot public school girls, but it wasn't worth it. I was eating that shitty food all the time and getting fat. I need a change.

June, 5, 1997

I can't take it anymore. I love Darcy more than anything. I sat down and wrote her this letter because I don't have the guts to ask her out. Seeing her at lunch every day is killing me. All these high school movies I watch end with the guy asking out the girl on the last day of school. It's cliché, but it makes sense. If she says "no," then you don't have to see her until the fall.

Dear Darcy,

I just want to say that I've liked you since the first day of school. I remember sitting in history class watching all the new faces pour into the classroom and your face stood out among them all. I kept looking at you all class hoping you would look back. I knew I should have talked to you as soon as I could, but I was shy and didn't have any confidence (I still don't!).

It was a miracle that you sat at our lunch table this year and we were able to become friends. It tore my heart out every time I heard you talk about your boyfriends to Cecilia.

They never appreciated you like I would.

It's going to suck not seeing you at lunch every day. If you ever want to go out on a date this summer, name the time and place. I just got my license and my car is fixed up, ready to go.

Your friend,

Nic

I looked at the letter for a while, and then laughed at how creepy I sounded and how ridiculous it would be to give that to her. I crumpled it up and threw it out. It felt good to write, though, like some kind of therapy.

June 6, 1997

I hate reading; I absolutely hate it with a passion. Why did these teachers assign us books to read during the summer? We toiled away with homework and tests all year; leave us alone for three months. This is the third year in a row that we have "summer readings." This year they gave us: *A Day No Pigs Would Die, Shoeless Joe,* and *The Pearl.*
I got through the last two summers only reading the book *Night* by Elie Weisel. It was only a hundred some pages and actually really terrifying and good but the other five books I was able to avoid reading by getting

the Cliff Notes, watching the movies, or copying another kid's paper. I don't even remember what they were; I think *A Separate Peace* was one of them. I read 10 pages and decided it was a snooze-fest. I did whatever I could to not turn a page. I don't know why, maybe I have ADD or something. I just get bored after reading for a few minutes. Years of television and video games have ruined my attention span.

I did read in grade school when we had the "Book it" program. That actually worked. I couldn't wait to read and get my sticker on my pin and then my free pizza from Pizza Hut. They need that for high school; I don't care if it's childish. Pizza spans all ages.

This summer is going to be different; I decided I'm going to read all three books. It's time to give a shit. For too long I just floated on by, not trying or caring about anything. *The Pearl* is only 100 some pages, so I'm going to start with that. They told us all through school to do the hardest assignment first, while you had the most energy and then when you were drained, the easy assignments would be waiting for you last.

In theory, this sounds great, but it didn't work for me. I had to do the easy stuff first. It made me feel like I was making a dent in my homework. If I sat for two hours working on something hard, I would be looking at all the other stuff I had to do after. So, if I got them out of the way first, then I could focus on the difficult assignment. This is how my brain works. I still think summer reading is bullshit. Give us time to rest our minds and use our bodies. Summer isn't for sitting around, it's for living, damn it!

June 6, 1997

Free! Finally free!! There's nothing better than coming home and knowing you won't have to go back to school for three months. God, what a rush! No more waking up at 6:00 in the morning or math class or having to see Darcy and her boyfriend in the hallway.

Driving home today, I put on *School's Out* by Alice Cooper on my *Dazed and Confused* CD and blasted it at full volume. It was amazing!

I'm going to miss having lunch with Darcy. That was the one time of day that I got to talk to a girl. She's going to the shore all summer while I'll be sweating in a hot truck, delivering auto parts. I'm so jealous. At least I will make some money and can buy some CD's and movies. That's really all I have in my life right now.

June 7, 1997

My first day at Earl's Auto Parts was pretty cool. I showed up, and a bunch of the guys from Lindsburg were there, so I was immediately comfortable. That didn't last long. They all started to bust my balls about anything and everything. Vince, Ralph's brother, started calling me names and then his friend Ski started making weird noises at me. His name really isn't Ski but that was his nickname for some reason. I have no idea why, but he is a pretty strange dude, so the name kind of fit him. Strange meaning he was always making jokes and noises with his mouth. I could definitely see him on SNL someday. I didn't know what to do when he started quacking like a duck at me, so I just laughed. He kept doing it, trying to get some reaction out of me until another driver came back from a delivery and then he started to harass him. Those guys are so strange.

They put me in a truck with an old guy and he drove delivering parts while I watched. It was a freaking amazing job. He could go wherever he wanted as long as he was back within a decent amount of time.

Here's how the job worked:

1) A garage is working on a car and needs a part
2) The garage calls Earl's and places an order
3) The part is pulled, and I'm told to deliver the part
4) I drive out and deliver the part and drive back

That was it, there were no worries about my drawer being light or cleaning the bathrooms or drive-thru people yelling at me. It was cake.

If the boss gave you a long run, like a half hour away, you could milk it and take some back roads or stop off at a convenience store and get some food. Some of the trucks had air conditioners and CD players, so you could listen to whatever music you wanted. They were hard to get though. The older guys all picked them first. I had to work my way up to get one of those.

There were some real wierdos who worked there. They were mostly older guys who were retired or just doing it as a part-time weekend job. The one guy I only saw for a day because the boss caught him for a second time drinking in the truck. He fired him on my second day. There's this one guy they call Hot Dog and he's this super old fart who wears one glove on his right hand. I asked Ralph why he did that, and he told me he uses it to wipe his nose. Ralph then said I should never take the old black truck, because the steering wheel is full of his boogers. Nasty!

Another character that works there is the guy named Pete Roy who looks like a human muskrat. He's short, skinny, has messed up teeth, bottle cap glasses, smells like cigarettes and has stringy red hair and horribly pale, reddish skin. I can't even tell how old he is; he could be 30 or he could be 60. He mostly works in the back of the store pulling parts for the drivers.

Pete is always pissed off. I don't blame him; the high school kids pick on him relentlessly. I never say anything bad about him. How could I? We get along good, I think he knows that I won't join in with the teasing. It doesn't help that his wife is 300 pounds. He is just a sad sack who screwed up in life. I hope I don't end up like that.

I'm just so glad I have a new job now. One that I really enjoy. It doesn't even feel like work because I just show up and then drive around in the truck all day, listening to music. I love being alone like that; it gives me time to think. It's also nice seeing so many girls running around in skimpy outfits in the nice weather. I wish I could do this job for the rest of my life.

June 10, 1997

I had heard of this guy Stanley Kubrick a while ago. I don't know much about him other than the fact that he directed *The Shining* with Jack Nicholas back in the 70's. The wrap on him is that his best movie is something called *2001: A Space Odyssey.* It came out in 1968 and is a science fiction movie. I haven't watched many old movies like that. My dad loves the old show called *Lost in Space*. It's this cheesy show that follows a family that's traveling around in space and their ship gets destroyed. They're trapped on some distant planet, and they run into weird aliens. The original effects are sooooo bad.

I was hesitant at first to rent *2001: A Space Odyssey* but my curiosity overcame me.

The movie opened with some apes in what looks like a prehistoric time. Then, a black statue shows up out of nowhere, and they start bashing each other's brains in. I was confused and thought the store gave me the wrong tape. Suddenly the movie cuts to some futuristic time on a space ship. Ok, I thought, here we go.

The story started off with potential. Some astronauts find the same black statue from the beginning buried on the moon. Very cool! I wondered how it got there and when the aliens would show up.

They never did.

The rest of the movie was about these astronauts going to Jupiter and some talking computer on the ship that tries to kill them. That was it. The ending didn't even make sense. I was so pissed that I wasted $2.59 and almost three hours of my life on it.

Don't get me wrong, the effects were super cool. I assume they were ground breaking for 1968. It wasn't like *Lost in Space* at all. The problem was the damn story. It was so freaking vague. I was lost half the time and the last 20 minutes was like some strange silent art movie. If you want to watch a real sci-fi movie, go rent *Aliens* or *Aliens 2*. Both are vastly superior to this thing.

There was a trailer on the beginning of the tape for another film Kubrick made called *A Clockwork Orange*. It looked really creepy. I couldn't tell what it is about but I hope it has a regular story.

2001 Space Odyssey: 2/5 stars

June 28, 1997

Every year, we go to the same beach town in New Jersey. We've been going there since I was born. This year is no different. The place is called Seaside Heights. My parents won't go anywhere else; I think they have obsessive compulsive disorder or something. I don't mind though, it's a nice town. They have a cool boardwalk with games and arcades. They don't have many arcades around my town so it's fun to play some of those old classics like Pac-Man, Q-Bert, and Punch-Out!! I like it because it reminds me of my childhood, when life was simple.

We usually rent the same house too. That's how

much my parents hate change. My dad loves to bring the same movies and TV shows to watch while we're there. *Lost Boys* is one of his favorite movies, and we watch it every year at the shore. I love that movie. I think most vampire movies are kind of stupid and hokey, but *Lost Boys* rules. It stars Jason Patric, Kiefer Sutherland, Corey Haim and Corey Feldman. What a cast! It is like an 80's rock and roll vampire movie, which is pretty cool.

I've never been much of a beach person. I get bored just lying around in the sun doing nothing. I can't swim, so I don't really go in the ocean. I just sit in the sand and have the water come up over my waist. That's fun for about 20 minutes, and then I'm ready to go. I do like to see the pretty girls in bikinis. I just wish I was with my friends down there; it's kind of awkward trying to secretly check them out when my mom isn't looking.

My sister came down with her female college friend as well. They didn't sit with us though. They went to the other end of the beach because they didn't want to be seen with our parents. I understand that. I guess I'll do the same thing when I'm in college, if I even go. College seems like a pipedream at this point, what would I even major in?

My favorite thing to do at the shore is crabbing. I'm pretty sure I have ADD so crabbing is right up my alley. My dad has about 10 metal traps that we tie chicken drumsticks inside and then we throw them out in the bay. You wait about 5-10 minutes and then pull them in. New Jersey has blue claw crabs that can get pretty big. I once got pinched by one on my finger and it was the most painful thing ever! It started bleeding and hurt the rest of the day. My dad showed me how to pick them up by the back swimmer apparatus, and I never made that mistake again.

After a few hours of crabbing, we would have a whole five gallon bucket full. We would take them home, and my dad would boil them all in a big pot and stink up the whole house. He used Old Bay spice, so it actually smelled kind of good. I didn't eat them though; watching my dad tear into a crab looked disgusting.

At night, we would go to the boardwalk and play all types of carnival games and cranes. I loved the crane games the most. I was so good at snagging stuffed animals, T-shirts, and other pointless prizes. It was more the challenge that interested me. Sometimes, I would spend five bucks to win a stupid little toy. It was nice going there, because I never saw anybody from my school. They were all at Ocean City or Wildwood. Darcy's parents had a place in Avalon, which is a ritzy beach town in Jersey. I would be horrified if anybody saw me walking around with my parents.

By the end of the week I was always out of clean clothes, out of money, and had a good tan. It was time to go home. I usually dreaded going back home but not this year. I have a sweet new summer job, and I'm ready to get back to kicking. I feel my leg getting weaker by the day. It needs some exercise! Two more months until tryouts!

Lost Boys: 4/5 stars

June 29, 1997

Ronnie, Ralph, Chuck, and I went to the movies tonight. They had been showing a trailer for this one called *Face-off*. I thought it looked like a stupid action movie, but Chuck said it was going to be good. Chuck loved those kinds of movies. I think it's because he smokes so much pot and the explosions dazzle the eye. It didn't matter to me; I would go see any movie. As long as I get to leave my house and hang out with people, I'll have a good time.

The movie starred Nicholas Cage and John Travolta. And the movie was as ridiculous and stupid as I thought. John Travolta plays an FBI agent who changes faces with the bad guy, who's played by Nicholas Cage. Then the FBI agent, as the bad guy, goes into prison to get some information about a bomb or something. I don't know, the story was hard to follow and I really didn't care why he was doing what he was doing. I just know the FBI agent's kid died and Nicholas Cage's character was responsible. I would make a bad film reviewer, that for sure.

The action scenes were cool, and the woman in the movie was really hot, so it wasn't all bad. Of course, the guys loved it. Action is my least favorite genre. Car chases and explosions kind of bore me. That why Tarantino is so good, he has a ton of violence, but the dialogue is really good, and it keeps you interested. He has a new movie coming out at the end of the year called *Jackie Brown*. Uggh. I can't wait that long!

Face-off: 2/5 stars

July 2, 1997

Now that vacation is over I starting to work more at Earl's. I work three days during the week, 10 hours a day, and 8 hours on Saturday. It's like a full time job! I'm making some good money though. I have to now because once football starts in August, I won't be able to work. Well, that is *if* I make the team. The kicking is still on track; I can't get out to the field as much but I still kick against the shed for at least 15 minutes a day.

It is nice driving around all morning though. At first, I hated it. That is until I started listening to Howard Stern. He's this crazy radio DJ who lives in New York. I don't know much about him but his radio show is absolutely insane. He has a whole team of wacky characters and is constantly having porn stars on the air. I've never heard anything like it.

He also has a group of mentally handicapped people called "the wack pack." Most of them have some kind of issue that makes them unable to fit into the rest of society. There is this guy Elephant Boy, who can barely speak, Crackhead Bob, who is like a retarded person because he smoked too much crack and a whole slew of others I can't think of right now. I love the show; he keeps me laughing all morning long.

The rest of the day kind of drags if I have a shitty truck with no CD player. I noticed the radio play's the same songs and bands over and over. Pink Floyd, Metallica, Nirvana, Pearl Jam, and Led Zeppelin. They never play any cool songs that weren't hits either, it's always the same hits. I even heard one station playing the same Pearl Jam song as another station, at the same time!

Sometimes I like to drive by McDonald's when I'm bored and see who is working the drive thru. I feel so glad I quit that soul sucking job whenever I drive by and see Marshall handing a bag out the drive thru window.

July 13, 1997

While I was driving around delivering auto parts on Saturday, I decided to stop at Dairy Queen and get some ice cream. It's been really hot lately and the truck I was driving that day didn't have any air conditioning. So why am I writing about this? Well I ran into Darcy and Cecilia! They were both sitting in Dairy Queen completely stoned eating ice cream. I didn't even see them; they saw me and yelled out to me from the back of the restaurant "Yo Nic!"

It was the middle of the day and they were so out of it. Darcy's parents don't make her work. I thought that's stupid because she's so bored, and then smokes weed all day to pass the time.

"So what have you been up to?" Darcy asked.

"Just working right now. It's a sweet job, I can do pretty much whatever I want; the boss doesn't care." I said pointing to my truck.

"Wow, that's awesome!" Cecilia said. "You should take us for a drive!"

"Haha, hell no. I can't lose this job. What have you guys been up to?" I said.

"Nothing much, This town sucks. You've got to do a good amount of drugs to make it fun around here. I had been at the shore since school ended but my mom got annoying so I came home for a week."

"You still going to the Page/Plant concert next week?" I asked.

"Oh yea, we are going to be there. I might be able to get some acid. Do you want any?"

"Holy shit. Nah, I'm good, that shit scares me."

"You're scared of everything."

She was spot on with that remark.

"Did you tell him the big news?" Cecilia asked Darcy.

Darcy looked confused, like she couldn't process what she was saying. Then Cecilia mouthed something to her, and then it was a like bulb came on in her clouded brain.

"Oh yea, me and Matt broke up for good this time!" Darcy said. "I'm so done with that guy, what an asshole."

"Thank God." I said. "Yea, never trust those baseball players. Bad news."

"He's going to college anyway, so there is no way it would have worked. I'm staying single for the rest of the summer, it's so much easier."

Cecilia looked at me and rolled her eyes. With that one look, it was like we were talking to each other mentally:

"Isn't Darcy such a spoiled brat?" - Cecilia
"I know. How are you friends with her?" - Me
"We've been best friends since we were five; it's

whatever now. Probably the same reason you are friends with Jerry."- Cecilia

"Do you think she'll ever see anything in me?"- Me

"Who knows, she has such a random taste in guys, I never know what is going on in her head."- Cecilia

It must be nice to take a break from dating like that, I thought. Darcy has such an easy life. A big house, a pool, a shore house, no job and boyfriends whenever she wants, it's not fair. She would never know the torture that I go through on a daily basis.

We talked for another five minutes, and then I told her I hoped to see her at the concert. She gave me a hug, and then I got my ice cream and went back to work.

I was actually feeling good for most of the summer getting ready for football not thinking about her. I wish I hadn't seen her; it was easier to keep her out of my mind when I hadn't seen her. Now, she's back in my head and I can't get her out!

July 14, 1997

So, I started reading *The Pearl* by John Steinbeck and I couldn't put it down. I read it in three days. Who would have thought? It's an amazing story of these native people who dive for pearls to support their families. The main native guy finds the biggest pearl in the world one day, and he thinks it'll change his whole life. Well, it does change his life but not for the better. It turns out that having a giant pearl that's priceless ruins his life.

I think it's an analogy for winning the lottery. I see people on the news who win the lottery and then go broke in a few years because they overspend and people keep asking them for money. It seems like kind of a government scam to get welfare checks back from poor people. They give them all this hope for winning and they buy into it. The scratch-offs are kind of fun, but I never win anything more than a dollar.

I'm not sure what I'm going to read next, *Shoeless Joe* or *A Day No Pigs Would Die*. They're both longer which really sucks.

July 20, 1997

I can now say I've been to a concert. And what a show! Well, from what I saw of the concert, it was so fun!

The day started off so well. I met Ralph and his brother Vince, and his goofy friend Ski in the back alley behind his house around 3:00. The show didn't start until 8:00, but the guys wanted to get to the parking lot super early, so we could tailgate. I had never heard of such a thing. I thought tailgate meant that you drove close to person in front of you. Ralph explained that tailgating was parking your car near the concert and the whole parking lot drinks beer and smokes pot. *How cool*, I thought.

Vince drove us to the concert in his tan 1986 Oldsmobile Cutlass Supreme. It was one of those cool

80's cars that had the cloth interior and was boxy all around. It was a total beater; I loved it. On the way there, Vince sparked a joint and we passed it around. The other people on the highway must have seen smoke bellowing out of the windows. I was constantly looking around for police officers while nobody else seemed to care.

When we got to the parking lot, there was a sea of cars trying to get in. The concert was at a big venue I think 15-20 thousands seats so the cars had to go somewhere. After about 25 minutes of traffic, we finally got in the parking lot and drove around until we found Vince's other friends who had already started drinking. They all had graduated with Vince in June and were going to car mechanic school together in the fall. They were total bad asses.

The parking lot was pretty sweet; all I heard were car radios blasting Led Zeppelin and could smell weed blowing all around. It looked like paradise. What a sight!

I stood around the crowd of guys for about five minutes and then one of the guys with a shaved head and tattoos said "don't just stand there, grab a beer!" I was relieved he told me to get one; I didn't want to just go and grab a beer without asking. Those guys were all older and tougher than I was. They were all gearheads like Vince was, but they had a look about them like they came out of jail. I went and got a beer and took a sip and stood there next to Ralph, watching them all talk. I didn't know what else to do.

15 minutes later, they all decided that the drinking needed to be escalated. "Let's do shotguns!"

the one guy yelled. What the hell is that, I thought. Then another guy started handing out fresh beers even though I was still working on my first beer.

"What are we doing?" I asked Ralph.

Vince came over and demonstrated what a shotgun was. He poked a hole in my can with his car key and told me to open the top and suck down the beer through the keyhole. It seemed really stupid. Why would we do this when I can just drink it normally?

"Ok, everybody get ready," shaved-head guy said. "1...2...3...drink!"

I did what he said; I put the keyhole to my mouth and opened the beer at the top. The cold, crisp beer rushed into my mouth like a waterfall. It was delicious. I was able to take down the whole beer in less than 20 seconds! I still didn't like the taste of beer, yet was able to chug it with no problem.

"Holy shit! " I said.

"Right? Shotguns will get you fucked up." Vince said.

We continued to drink for the next hour, doing a few more shotguns. I think I was at 5 beers, which was getting into the danger zone for me. I was starting to get drunk, that was for sure. Then, out of nowhere, Darcy showed up with Cecilia.

"Hey Nic!" Darcy screamed with a red plastic cup in one hand and a cigarette in the other.

"Woah, how did you find us?" I asked in a surprised tone.

"We've been walking around, getting free beer from different people. Beats having to pay for it."

"Here, let me fill you up," I said.

I went and grabbed two more, one for Cecilia as well.

"You guys should walk around the parking lot - crazy people everywhere," Cecilia said. "We saw a bunch of old guys on LSD; they were out of their minds."

"Yea and people got beer pong setup, and a guy s selling balloons of nitrous on that side," Darcy said pointing towards the fence.

"Oh man, I might have to buy one of those balloons," I said.

Whenever I saw Darcy outside of school, it was like a dream. She was looking better than ever with her Led Zeppelin shirt half cut so you could see her belly and two French braided pony tails. At least I was kind of drunk, and all my nerves were calm. I don't remember what we talked about but I do remember her laughing a lot. I'm good at making her laugh, like I'm a lowly jester. Then she'll move on to her king.

The girls stuck around for about a half hour, and then she gave me a hug and went back to walking around the parking lot. It must be nice being a pretty girl walking around, and guys just give you free drinks, I remember thinking as they walked away. That would never happen to me.

Well, what happened after they left was a giant fog in my brain. I know we kept pounding beer after beer until one of Vince's friends had about 10 nitrous filled balloons in his hand. He handed them out, and we all sucked them down. It was the last thing I needed. I could barely speak after inhaling that junk. Then it was time to go into the show. I remember stuffing a beer in my pocket and then walking in a crowd of people to the venue. We found our seats and then...nothing.

I woke up at some point during the show with puke all over my shirt. I mean covered, absolutely drenched. It was disgusting. I took off my shirt, and then I needed to take a piss. So in my drunken state, I climbed up above a wall and into the box seats. I didn't realize what I was doing until the day after when I thought about it. I was in luxury seats that people paid a lot of money for. I found the private bathroom, took a piss and then climbed back down. The people in them must have been mortified. I'm just lucky that I didn't get arrested.

It was the perfect timing because the song *Whole Lotta Love* had just started, and I stood in the center of the seats and banged my head like I did in my room alone so many nights. They left the stage, and I was sad because the show was over and I only got to hear one song. The stage was dark, but everyone was still cheering. The people weren't leaving.

Five minutes later, the band came back out and the crowd got even louder. What was that about? Then, they played one of my favorite underplayed radio songs *Thank You* and ended with *Rock and Roll*. It was beautiful seeing those two legends up there on the stage. I didn't even care that I missed the whole show. I was glad I woke up just in time for the last three songs. I asked Ralph what was up with them leaving the stage at the end, and he said it's called an encore. He said it's normal for bands to do that at the end of a concert.

What an experience! Now I want to go to another one. I'm so tired today; I'm going to bed early tonight

July 22, 1997

So I found out that the book I have to read, *Shoeless Joe*, is a movie! The movie is called *Field of Dreams* and was released in 1989. I hadn't even heard of it before. Apparently, it was a big deal when it came out and it stars Kevin Costner and James Earl Jones, who was the famous voice behind Darth Vader. I wish movie trivia was a class in school; I would ace it.

I really did try reading the book, but it was kind of boring. Instead, I went out to Blockbuster and rented the tape. Two hours later and I was all done. *Field of Dreams* was just ok. I don't know why it was up for a best picture Oscar to be honest. Kevin Costner and James Earl Jones did a good job; I just thought it was a little cheesy. I get that it's a fantasy movie, but I thought it was dumb that these baseball player ghosts came back to some field this guy builds on his farmland. It was entertaining; I will say that, so it wasn't all bad.

After I watched the movie, I then went back and tried the book again. This time, I could picture the main character as Kevin Costner, and it made it easier to read. I don't know why. I probably just watch too much TV and it has taken away my imagination. Either way, it worked, and I was able to skim my way through the book and get a good gist of it. My trick was to read every fifth page. The other ones I glance at, looking for certain events that happened in the movie. The movie and the book are close, but definitely not identical.

Since football tryouts are approaching, I decided to jump right into *A Day No Pigs Would Die*. So far, I know it's about a kid who lives on a farm back in old times, the early 1900's, I think and the neighbor gives the kid a baby piglet to raise. It's a nice book so far, it reminds me of when we got our dog, Marley, as a puppy. I love Marley; he's one of my best friends. Other than, that I don't know where this book is going, story wise.

Field of Dreams: 3/5 stars

July 25, 1997

I went out fishing with Ralph today, him and me. His brother, Vince, found this really cool farm pond out in the sticks. Vince caught two big lunker bass out of there last week, so we decided to check it out. It's pretty cool because the owner doesn't care that we fish; he just has a rule that we throw them back.

It was really hot today, so we waited until about 7:00 to go out. The summers here are great, it gets dark around 9:00. If you go out at dusk, the bass come out from their holes and jump for top water lures. That is my favorite type of fishing. I love running a big jitterbug to catch bass. A jitterbug is a lure that looks like a big black bug that makes a lot of noise on the top of the water.

I picked up Ralph in my El Camino and we drove down there, gas blazing and the 350 small block roaring. Nobody could stop us. A small victory for us losers. I loved driving away from it all.

When it was just Ralph and me, we would talk and we would get kind of deep about our lives. It was kind of like we were our own therapists. There was so much going on in our heads that when we got stoned and hung out, everything was on the table. I sparked a joint when we got to the pond, and the flood gates opened.

I told him for the first time about trying out for the football team. I told him I had been practicing in secret this whole time and in a few days, I was going to try and make the team.

"You're serious?" he asked looking stunned.

"Dead," I said.

"Haha, no way. Hahaha."

He looked at the sky and kept laughing.

"Shut up!" I said feeling kind of betrayed.

"Sorry, but do you really think you can do it?"

"Dude, I've been practicing every day since December; I can definitely kick."

"Wow, if you can pull it off it'll be amazing. I can't wait to tell Ronnie and Jerry."

"No, don't say anything. I want to surprise them."

"Yea, good move. That'll be hilarious."

We then fished some more and bitched and moaned about people in school, girls, our parents, and life in general. We both agreed it really sucks around our area, and after graduation we should move somewhere else. That's what I like about smoking pot, it opens your mind to other things.

When we were high, it seemed so rational that we could go on the road after we graduate. We could just get in his 1987 Buick Regal and drive away across the country and start a new life. We could go to some city where nobody knows us and re- invent ourselves. It's so hard to change your life when everybody already knows you.

As I write this, the pot has worn off, and nothing about our plan makes any sense. How would we support ourselves? We have no money. Where would we possibly go to make a new life? We have no skills. I'll probably end up going to college, and Ralph will probably be a carpenter or something. Maybe after that, we can get out of this damn town.

August 3, 1997

Tomorrow is the first day of football try outs. I'm so nervous. Am I really going to do this? I hope so.

I went out to the baseball field for possibly the last time today. It was 95 degrees and the grass was dead as hell. The ground was dry and perfect for kicking. I setup a football around 50 times and booted most of them over the backstop. I got home and took a shower, and got ready for bed around 9:00, which is super early for me. Tryouts start at 8:00 sharp, and I want to get as much sleep as possible.

There's nothing stopping me now but myself. I've folded under pressure my whole life, but this time, I can't. I've kicked so much the last eight months that it's automatic now. I just worry about all the eyes on me. The eyes of the football jocks. They'll think you're a loser anyway, so what do you have to lose?

Ok, time to go to bed. I doubt I'll be able to sleep.

August 4, 1997

I just got back from tryouts. I got home a little bit ago and took a shower and am the most excited I've ever been! I haven't been happy many times in my life, and today, well, today is one of those days. My life feels like it's about to change forever.

I woke up more nervous than I've ever been. I didn't even sleep last night; I just tossed and turned and chewed my fingers thinking about how everything I had worked for was coming down to one day. The coach didn't even know I was coming.

I just showed up with my bright blue El Camino and my cleats. That was it. I sat in the car for a while before I went out. I almost just drove back home thinking to myself "maybe next year."

In the end I got out and walked over to the team that was gathered around the coach. They all had pads and practice jerseys on because they were all on the team already. I was the only one who was new. Not many kids start to play football their junior year. The freshmen have their own team, and then they go up to junior varsity in their sophomore year, and then varsity junior or senior year. Some guys never make it to varsity because they suck. Our school is small so we don't have tryouts; everybody makes the team, but not everyone will play. Kind of like soccer.

I wasn't like the others; I had a specialized skill that they didn't. As I walked up to the team, I could feel myself starting to panic. I knew I was good, but like with soccer, I was worried what people thought of me. It's my main character flaw, and there is nothing I can do about it.

I stood in the back, as Coach Turner, who's an English teacher, looked at his clipboard. Coach Turner is an old school guy with a big belly and gray hair. I think he is only in his 50's, but he looks older. I heard he was in one of the wars, but I'm not sure which one. The guys were all talking and goofing around. I looked around and saw Jerry and Vince standing next to each other and I felt so much better. I went over and pushed Jerry in the back.

"Yo fucker!" I said pushing him.

"Dude, what are you doing here?" he asked with a confused look on his face.

"Trying out man. Fuck soccer, I'm gonna kick a football now."

"Really? Wow. We need a kicker. Brad is ok, but he missed a bunch last year. He doesn't even practice kicking that much, he's more of a cornerback."

"What's your range?" Ronnie asked.

"I can do 45 right now. I want to get up to 50 one day."

"Holy shit, that's great!"

The coach then yelled for everyone to be quiet, like a drill sergeant would. He then gave a long speech about football. I really don't remember much; I kind of zoned out while he was talking. I tend to do that if it's not about movies or television or video games or girls.

After his speech, he saw me standing there and asked who I was and what I wanted. I told him that I wanted to try out to be the kicker, and then he rolled his eyes and said "Soccer player?" I said not anymore and he said "Good answer. We don't want two sport players on this team." Everyone laughed, and then he told me to go with the assistant coach, Coach Wade, and show him what I could do while he took the rest of the team to the other side of the field.

The assistant coach was mainly involved with the special teams. He's a lot different from Coach Turner. He's skinny and younger and does everything he's told. I felt safer when I was told to go with him. Coach Turner kind of scares me.

So there's the offense, defense, and the special teams on a football team. The special teams squad was strictly for kickoffs, field goals and punts. Most of the guys on the special teams are the worst players. The coach does that because he doesn't want his best players getting hurt on kickoffs. It makes sense.
Coach Wade started us out stretching for about 20 minutes, and then we ran around the field I don't know how many times. Running is the absolute worst. I'm really fast and probably could be a great track star, but I absolutely, positively despise running. All I thought the whole time was "Why do I have to do this? I won't be running in the game." I think it's that team mentality the

coaches try to instill in us. I get it. The problem is that I'm a loner and will always be a loner. The whole team spirit bullshit never fit with my personality. That's why kicking is for me. I do my job and that's it. Nobody else is responsible. I'll run with them and practice with them but in reality, I'm a team of one.

Finally, an hour later, Coach Wade says to me "Ok, let's see what you got." He then called the backup quarterback over to hold the ball. As I was lining up, I thought I should be nervous, but I wasn't for some reason. Maybe because when I took three steps back and two steps over, I was in my comfort zone. It felt like I was back on the baseball field, all by myself. Everything around me disappeared.

Coach Wade started me at the 8 yard line, which is a joke. That amounts to a 25 yard field goal. This is because you add on 10 yards for the end-zone and 7 yards for the snap of the ball. 8 yards+17 yards = 25 yards. I drilled it with my eyes closed. Then, we went to 35, again, right on through. "Ok, hot shot, 40 now," he said. I lined up, and again, I nailed it.

"That's my limit for now," I said to the coach. I didn't want to chance anything higher.

He clapped and smiled after the last kick and then told me I had potential. He said I would still need to work because kicking in a real game would be totally different. There would be crowd noise, more pressure and 11 guys coming to rip off your head.

I don't care about any of that right now. All that matters is that I was invited back for another practice. I just hope I won't crack under pressure. It's hard not to think about my classmates watching me from the stands and judging me.

August 8, 1997

So I had a great week of kicking with Coach Wade and he told Coach Turner who said I'm officially on the team! He made it clear that I'm not the official kicker yet, but will be able to earn my spot if I keep doing well.

Now that it's official I'm on the team, I told my boss at Earl's that I couldn't work anymore. He was really nice and said I could stay on and just work Saturdays if I wanted. I said absolutely. I told him after the football season, I can go back to working during the week. Even though my paycheck is going to suck, it's still great that I get to keep the job. I definitely can't go back to McDonald's.

My mom and dad freaked out when I told them. I hadn't seen my dad so happy since I fixed up my El Camino. He was in disbelief. My mom even went out and bought me a football cake to celebrate. I tried to play it off as nothing. I hated being praised. How could I? I've been beaten down so many years that when something good happens, I'm waiting for the other shoe to drop.

As I was taking a shower after practice, I was able to secretly congratulate myself. That'll be the extent of my self-indulgence. It'll going to be a lot more work from here on in. I had so much to do. I'm just glad that

I'll be able to have a shot at something different.

August 10, 1997

Now that I was under Coach Wade's tutelage, I was learning how kicking really works. He explained to me that the first short step is called the "jab step." The reason for this is the shift your body weight forward, in the direction of the ball.

The second step is called the "drive step," and is executed by taking a long stride in the direction of the ball with your kicking foot.

The third step is taken by putting your plant foot to the side of the football. Coach Wade said this is the most important step.

"This will determine where your plant foot will anchor you to the field while you kick the ball," he said.

Apparently, my form had been all wrong. He gave me some pointers to get more power on the ball. He said my plant foot should be a few inches behind the ball to insure a better kick. My plant foot was landing next to the ball, and I wasn't getting the full amount of power.

He also showed me how to really boom kickoffs. He showed me that when I ran up and kicked the ball, my plant foot should go up in the air, and my whole body should be at a diagonal to the ball, which will give me the most power.

It took me about 20 tries, but I finally got it down, and it really works! I kicked a really good one that went almost 60 yards and into the end zone!

August 14, 1997

It's pretty awesome that I'm on the team, but these summer practices are horrible. They last all day, and it's been really hot. I'm so tired of running. I would rather be working at Earl's or at home watching TV in the air conditioning. I'm so jealous of Ralph because he's been working almost every day and is making a ton of money. I haven't even gone fishing in two weeks, and the summer is almost over.

It kind of sucks too, because nobody really talks to me. Outside of Jerry and Ronnie, it's kind of like soccer but more isolated. The soccer guys were a bunch of maniacs who got off on torturing us nerds, but the football guys don't seem to care. I prefer being ignored to being picked on. Still, it definitely wasn't what I envisioned they whole time I was practicing on my own. Really, what in life lives up to the expectations you have in your head? Not much. Even when we fantasize about having the summer off and doing all this cool shit, we usually just end up working and doing jack squat.

August 17, 1997

I watched a really sad movie on Saturday. It's called *Edward Scissorhands*. It stars this guy I haven't seen before named Johnny Depp. It was directed by Tim Burton who did *Beetlejuice* and *Batman*, so I assumed it had to be good. Oh, and Winona Ryder, who I remember from *Beetlejuice* is in it.

Johnny Depp plays this Frankenstein-type creature named Edward, that has scissors for hands. He wasn't supposed to have scissors for hands. A mad scientist who lived at the end of town in a big creepy mansion created him. As the scientist was getting ready to put his regular hands on him, he had a heart attack and died. They never explained where the scissors came from.

The movie started out good. Edward is discovered in his strange mansion on the hill by a local Avon sales lady and is taken into town when she finds out he's all alone. Initially most of the town accepts him as some eccentric person who can cut hair and trim hedges. Some people are suspicious though.

Winona plays the daughter of the Avon lady who Edward falls in love with.

Eventually, the townspeople start to take advantage of Edward and then turn on him. This is when the movie gets really sad. Edward can't talk, so he tries doing good things for people but ends up harming them with his scissor hands in the process. The people think he's dangerous and is trying to hurt them. A string of bad things happen, and the film ends with him back in his mansion, completely alone.

140

I really liked the movie, but it was hard to watch. Edward was so lonely and misunderstood, I felt like I was watching myself on the screen. He just wanted to help people, and they turned on him. It seems that's the way humanity works; they'll always turn on you if you're different, no matter what. It is so depressing. Even though I liked it, I don't think I can watch it again. I'll be thinking about Edward, alone in his mansion forever and ever.

Edward Scissorhands: 3.5/5 stars

August 26, 1997

"Yo man, when are you joining the sacristans?" Jerry asked me at practice today. "There are going to be some open spots since some of the seniors graduated."

"Nah, I hate that shit," I said.

Jerry had been a sacristan since freshman year; it was mostly football players and basketball players. Those two groups of people seemed to get along the best. I still didn't consider myself a football player; I was a kicker who wore a football jersey.

Jerry had high school figured out from the beginning. Even before the first class of freshman year, he had a leg up on Ralph and me. Since he played football, they started to practice in August and he got to meet a bunch of upperclassman. He was so extroverted and confident that they accepted him right away even though he was a freshman.

This was important because there were certain things you could do to get the most out of Lindsburg. The main thing the upperclassman football players taught him was to get very friendly with a certain priest. This poor priest was born with elephantiasis and his whole lower half was enormous. The first time I saw him walking down the hallway, I was baffled. His name was Father Thompson. He would walk the halls greeting the students with a big smile on his face. He was so nice. I don't know what his actual title is at the school, but he is in charge of the sacristans, who are kids who want to be involved with the church service. It's a lot like an altar boy. They hold crosses and light candles, stuff like that. I never even considered signing up for it. Why would I? I hated church. Jerry knew better. The older guys told him to join, and he took their advice. It was the best thing he could have done.

The reason was that Father Thompson was kind of a pushover. He would pretty much do whatever the football player sacristans told him. They would take total advantage of him by hanging out in his office, getting out of class to help him with errands around the school. They even convinced him to take a road trip to Philadelphia to see some churches. They ended up going to one church and then the rest of the time, they got cheesesteaks and walked around Center City.

Since Father Thompson was handicapped, the principal would let him do whatever he wanted. It was a perfect situation. The kids would pull his strings, and he would do what they said because he wanted to be liked. They were getting out of class at least once a week and it was approved!

Even though I had a free get out of class pass right in front of me, I knew it wasn't for me. I hated everything about church, and it wasn't worth the headache. Besides, I didn't really want to hang out with all those jocks. Jerry was my friend, but the other guys were kind of jerks. I wouldn't fit in.

August 27, 1997

So after a month of practicing with the team, I'm feeling so much better about kicking. We had a scrimmage against the junior varsity squad today, and I got to kick in a real game-like situation. I hit a 26 yard field goal and a 33 yard field goal! It was so awesome!

Our lineup is pretty much set for the season. I don't know all the positions though, only a few of the obvious ones

Quarterback - Jake Tanner
Running Back - Willie Humina
Wide Receiver - Todd Muler
2nd Wide Receiver - Jim Grayson
Linebacker - Jerry Romano
Tight End - Brad Swerty

I know the other guys names, but I'm unsure of their positions. Oh and I know the backup quarterback,

Ryan Mikal. He holds the ball when I kick it. Maybe by the end of the season, I'll know more of the positions and what they do, but for now that's all I can name. Probably not though, knowing me. The whole game of football is confusing as hell. There are so many plays, and the guys are running all around the field with an insane energy.

Coach Turner even had me do a fake field goal play, where I passed the ball instead of kicking it. I put a nice spin on the ball and made a perfect short 5 yard pass. The fake field goal is a trick play used on 4th down to get a first down. It seemed to work well in practice, but in a game, I can see it turning into a disaster if the other team picks up on it.

Jerry was telling me this was Jake's first season starting. He said he's not sure if he'll be good right away. He said it might take a few games for him to get in his groove.

August 29, 1997

So, I finished *A Day No Pigs Would Die,* and it was heartbreaking! It was such a pain to read and go to practice every day. I got it done though; I finished all three books before the summer is over. I still need to write the report on this; hopefully I can do this soon.

The basic story of the book is about a boy who got a baby pig and raised it. Eventually the pig became his best friend, and then he had to kill and eat the poor animal because it was barren and the family was starving and there wasn't any food. I was so upset. It was such a good book up until that point.

Later, I thought about it in contrast to the fucked up movies that I watched and it made sense that the pig had to die. I guess it makes it more real that way. If it ended on a happy note then it wouldn't be a good story.

Books are weird like that. I can watch a dozen films with unhappy endings and it won't affect me, but one book almost had me in tears. It's more personal, I think. You get to really feel a part of the characters, because you can see what they are thinking. Also, when you read, it takes longer and the greater amount of time spent with the characters creates a stronger bond. In a movie, you only get two hours with the characters, and when something happens to them, it's not as tragic to the viewer.

So, wow, another good book. If I wasn't so lazy I would read more. Reading is just so time consuming and quiet. I don't like the quiet of the room. Oh well. Maybe if I go to college, I can read more.

Oh, and they gave out the uniforms at practice today. Coach Wade said that kickers and quarterbacks usually wore a number below 10. It really didn't make sense that a rule would apply to two positions so different, but whatever. Since Jake took number 4, I had my pick of all the other numbers. I always loved number 8 for some reason, so I picked that.

It felt like a dream, holding that green Lindsburg football Jersey in my hand. It was bright and still had that new jersey smell. I'll have to do some dives in the grass to dirty it up, I thought.

September 1, 1997

It was the first day of school today, and I wasn't terribly depressed, like years before. It was a strange feeling. I was actually looking forward to seeing Darcy at lunch. I hadn't seen her since the concert and was wondering what her summer was like.

As I walked in the cafeteria, anxiety filled my whole body, I was afraid that Darcy would be sitting at a table with all new people. I stopped at the entrance and looked around the room for her. When I saw her sitting at the same table as last year, calmness washed over me. I hated change. Things should stay the same as long as possible. If something isn't broken, don't fix it.

I went and sat in my position at the table next to Ralph, across from Darcy, cattycorner to Cecilia and Greg. Bill was next to Ralph.

"Wow, you are tan!" Darcy said as I sat down.

"Yea, I've been out in the sun the last month. It's brutal."

"Why?"

"Football practice."

"Wait, what? Are you the ball boy now?"

"Almost, one step above. I'm the kicker now."

"Wow, that is crazy!" she said. "What made you want to do that?" she said.

"Well, it was your idea, don't you remember?" I said.

"Maybe, did I say something?"

"Yea, during study hall last year, after I quit soccer."

"Oh, haha, I was probably high."

"How is field hockey going?"

"I quit that shit. I only did it because my mom made me. My parents had a big blow up over the summer, so they don't really care what I do now."

"Really?"

"Yea, and they kicked out my brother. Fucking asshole got caught dealing," she said.

"Where is he living?"

"A friend's house for now. Guy needs to get a job, he's such a bum."

I don't know if I was seeing things, but it felt like Darcy wasn't looking at me like a loser anymore. It might have been because I didn't feel like a loser sitting in front of her at the lunch table. At first, I thought I could try to work this whole football team angle on her to make her like me. That meant I didn't need to make her laugh like I was a clown anymore. Well, that lasted about 10 minutes and then I was back to acting like a total goofball. My foolish personality was my default setting, and what made her talk to me in the first place. It made me happy to see her and Cecilia smile.

Even if this football experiment goes well, I don't think I'll ever be a ladies' man. Those guys have something I'll never have: the confidence that makes them *think* they belong even though they *know* they don't. That shit can't be taught or acquired, that is inborn.

September 5, 1997

    I hit the snooze for the first time in my life this morning. I'm writing this in fear on my bed. I don't want to get up. It's the morning of my first game, and I'm thinking about not going to school. I can't believe I got myself into this. I don't think I can do it. Our school has a policy that if you don't go to school on Friday, then you can't play in the game. I can't take the chance of making a fool of myself in front of all those people. I never do well under pressure. Fuuuuuck!

    I hit the snooze again. I smell the coffee maker downstairs and can hear the TV. Soon, mom is going to come up and get me. I have to make up an excuse now or go to school. Fuuuuck!

September 5, 1997 – Part 2

    So, I ended up getting up. I went to school like a good boy and couldn't concentrate all day. I was riddled with anxiety like never before. I thought about all those people looking at me under the lights. All the cool kids would be there. It would be an illuminated stage to show off how much of an idiot I'm.

    Since our school didn't have its own stadium, we had to take a bus to our home field. It was at a nearby public high school. We shared the stadium with them. If they had a home game, we were away and vice versa.

    I sat in the front of the bus by myself. Jerry said

148

to keep a low profile for a while and to not say much. He said I had to earn my way to the back of the bus. On the way to the stadium it was quiet, the coach didn't like horsing around before the game. Before we got off, he gave us a speech about how this was a new year and the seniors would have to set a good example, and that we had a fresh start. It was cliché coach talk. I just sat there and thought about not screwing up.

It was kind of cool walking onto the field. The stadium looked so big standing on the 50 yard line. We got there early to practice, so nobody was in the stands yet. There was still an hour to go until the game. We stretched out and then broke off into offense, defense, and special teams. I practiced kicking through the uprights for about 20 minutes. I hit all my kicks from 20-40 yards. The rest of the time, I just stretched on the sidelines and watched the cheerleaders practice their routines, and the stadium filled up in the meantime.

I looked toward the stands to see who was there. I was curious, so I looked up and there were Ralph, Bill and Greg all sitting together. I waved to them and they waved back. I must have looked like such a dork.

I also saw some of the soccer players and their girlfriends; they didn't seem to have a care in the world. As I was looking at them, Marshall Gomer caught me and stared at me dead in the eyes. Normally I would have looked away with fear, but I stared right back at him until he looked away. I was down on the field now, and he was in the stands. I was wearing a football uniform with brand new cleats. Yet, he still was dating one of the hottest girls in school, so he still won. It didn't bother me, I was used to it. I shook it off.

We won the coin toss and decided to kick first. That was a good strategy because in the second half we would get the ball first. So, if we stopped them on defense on the first drive, we would have an advantage.

There wasn't much pressure on kick offs. The ball was placed on the 40 yard line which was nice, because in the NFL, the ball is put on the 20 yard line. Most high school kickers can get it to the 20 yard line of the other team, a 40 yard kick, which is easy. I normally can kick anywhere from 50-60 yards.

Doing it in practice was one thing but with the lights and the crowd and my teammates looking at me, it was so different. I tried to block it all out by keeping my eyes on the ball and not looking at anybody. All I had to do was kick and then hang back and watch them tackle the returner. I took 11 steps back and 7 steps over. I did my hop and then a fast jog/walk to the ball and walloped it good. I hit it right in the middle of the ball. I looked up to see it flying through the air and it was caught at the 10 yard line. A perfect boot! The returner was crushed at the 15 yard line, and when I got to the sidelines, the guys smacked me on the head and yelled "yeeeeea!"

For most of the game I stayed on the sidelines. At the beginning of the fourth quarter we were up 21-3. I was happy that in my first game, I didn't have any pressure. My stomach was in knots at every 3rd down near the end zone. I wasn't eager to go out there and kick a field goal. I had to ease into this new role.

Near the end of the game, it was a fourth down and we had the ball on the 16 yard line. I was already warming up with the practice net. That was part of the routine; anytime the team got to the 25 yard line or closer, I would start to warm up.

Since we were up 21-17 and there were only 25 seconds left in the game, I assumed the coach would call an end zone pass or just knee the ball and run out the clock. Instead, he yelled "Walenti, let's see what you got!" I almost shit my pants. I ran out on the field with the special teams and lined up for the kick. It was a 33 yarder.

At least we had practically won the game already, so I wasn't nervous at all. I figured that if I gave it a good boot and it came close, I wouldn't look like an ass. They ball was snapped, and I hit it perfectly. The ball easily glided over the crossbar by a few feet, and it was good! I jumped up in celebration, like I won the Super Bowl. I looked towards the stands and nobody was paying attention. The parents section was clapping a little bit, but the students were all talking to each other.

I ran towards the sidelines and the coach grabbed my helmet "Great kick Walenti!" Then he let me go, and I waited on the sideline for the game to end.

When the bus got back to the school, Jerry said they were getting together at one of the guys' houses and having some beers. I told him that I was already meeting up with Ralph, Bill and Greg at the diner. He said "Ok, maybe after next game." I was so pissed! I never get invited anywhere, and I missed a golden opportunity to hang out with some cool kids. Still, I couldn't abandon my real friends who would be there regardless. Also, I was scared to drive around with beer on my breath. I didn't want to have even one and drive home. What if I got pulled over? My dad would kick my ass!

The diner was the right choice. I met up with them, and we ate cheese fries and talked about the weird stuff we talk about.

September 7, 1997

Whenever someone asks me what my favorite subject is, I tell them "Study Hall." It makes them laugh, but it's the truth. I really don't care about nor am I interested in any subject. I wonder if something is wrong with me. I like sports, cars, music, and television. School's so boring in comparison. I don't understand how some of these honor students do it.

I make sure to put a study hall on my roster every year. I never had detention, but I would assume study hall is very similar. You just sit there in silence and do school work or not. This year I'm trying to get my school work done instead of just doodling. It makes sense. Why not use the time to do my homework, so when I get home from practice at 7:30, I can eat dinner and watch TV until bed? Duh!

Now I look at the people who just goof around and draw or sleep and think they're stupid. Maybe they don't want people to see them doing homework and look like a dork? Or they were like me, not a care in the world. I can understand that. I still I just do enough to get by. If I tried harder, I think I could get B's or maybe even A's, but who knows.

What's strange to me is that all through grade school and into high school, getting good grades was seen as nerdy. It was like the cool people got together and determined that if you tried hard and got good grades, you would be an outcast. That was the way it worked since first grade. That's probably why I didn't try hard, to be honest. I wanted to be cool.

September 12, 1997

I always hated math. I barely made it through Algebra I in freshman year and now I'm in Algebra II. It's stupid that they gave us a year off with Geometry and now we need to remember how to do Algebra again. Numbers in general bother me. I hate seeing a bunch of them on the page of a book or on a chalkboard. It looks like nonsense. Why do we need to learn this?

Our teacher is Mr. Howard, who is a complete dick. He's this older guy who has a big belly, receding hairline, and always wears a tie with a flat end (instead of the usual triangle). I don't know why, but that bothers me. I show up to class every day hoping he'll throw in a triangle tie once in a while, but it never happened.

He has this way of talking slow and deliberate, like we are dumb. It's an obvious way of making fun of us right in front of our faces. When he asks a question and nobody wants to answer, he has this one line he says:

"Have you guys been sucking on the tailpipe of a

bus today?"

It wasn't even funny the first time. But he keeps saying it. I'm convinced he's just bored with his job, hates kids, and is just playing mind games with us.

The worst part about Algebra was that we had to "show our work" when we solved problems. I didn't know how to solve problems though. I never paid attention or even cared. Since Mr. Howard gave us take home tests, I had this trick to pass the tests. I would get some of answers from a smart person in the class, and then I would make up "fake" work to show how I got the answer. It was all nonsense. I just put in some letters and numbers, and made it look legitimate.

The first time I did it, I thought I would get caught, but he just looked at the circled correct answer at the bottom and then the mess of work and then put a C on the paper. I only got enough answers to get a C. I guess I could have gotten all the answers but I was lazy. Also, an A is kind of obvious when you're cheating. C is good enough for me. Hey, that rhymes!

We have this girl Jaime O'Bannon in my class who's a stone cold bitch. She's kind of hot, in a crack addict kind of way, and is dating that stoner Jack Cleasock. She walks around the halls with a scowl on her face acting like she's better than everyone.

On Monday, she and Mr. Howard had it out. It had been building for a while, actually since the first day of class, when she wanted to sit next to her friend and Mr. Howard told her no. They squabbled for a few minutes until Jaime finally gave up. Ever since then, he's been baiting her with little digs. She finally had enough.

I don't really know what started it, because whenever Mr. Howard lectured about Algebra, I zoned out and would just draw in my copy book. All I remember was Jaime standing up and yelling at him. I looked up and he was telling her to sit down. She yelled back saying that she wanted to switch classes. He told her to sit down in his calm creepy voice. She got louder, and he told her to sit down calmly. She started to cry and said "I can't take this class anymore!" That's when his eyes bulged out and he actually yelled, "Then get the fuck out!"

It was crazy. She ran out down the hall. I don't even know where she went. Mr. Howard just went to the door, closed it, and went back to his calm creepy voice, talking about math. It was then I knew he was a complete lunatic. Jaime is no better, she's a terrible person. She hasn't been back in class since Monday, so I assume she got her class changed.

September 13, 1997

We had our 2nd game on yesterday. It was our first away game. I was nervous because we had to take the bus. I hadn't been on a school bus since April and did not want to get back on one. I have that thing the soldiers had when they came back from the Vietnam war. I think it's called PTSD. I don't know what it stands for, but that is what I have when I see a school bus.

It mostly stemmed from being on the soccer

team. When we had to travel to another school to play, it was like *Lord of the Flies* on that bus. There's something about being on a bus outside of school hours and off of school property that makes kids act like lunatics. I had seen this behavior in the past when we went on field trips, and guess what? The soccer fools were no exception. As soon as the bus took off, and we were a mile down the road, the hazing started.

It started with ear flicking and then would move on to name calling, smacks to the back of the head and wet willies, and I even saw a freshman get some water poured on him after a night game on the ride home. It was awful. I tried to hide like I did with the normal bus ride home but it was harder because the bus was full. The front of the bus filled up quick, so if you got anywhere near the back, it was torture-town.

One time on the bus, I reached my boiling point. The endless teasing was going on as usual, and I was slumped in my seat, trying to hide from everyone. Marshall Gomer started talking nasty sexual shit about my mom.

"Nic's mom is such a whore!"

A guy named Jimmy P., who was this muscular Italian guy chimed in as well.

"Yea, she sucks so much cock," he said.

I couldn't believe what I was hearing. Why oh why? I hated Jimmy more than Marshall, he was a cocky mother fucker. I had enough.

"Yea, well I banged your mom last night!" I said to Jimmy P. I couldn't believe I said it. It was a really stupid line, but it was all I could think of.

"Oh shit, you wanna go?" he yelled as he motioned for me to fight him.

I went to stand up, and he clocked me in the head. I was so enraged I couldn't even feel it and I speared him in the chest. I got a couple of really good body shots as he punched my back. A few seconds later, the assistant coach pulled me off. The coach knew how much I got teased, and he didn't even scold me. He yelled at the whole bus and didn't let us talk the rest of the bus ride. I felt great though. I wasn't sure if Jimmy was going to try and kick my ass at a later date. He never did; I scared him. The rest of the season, nobody talked to me, it was like a shunning. I preferred it though; there was no more teasing after that.

The football bus wasn't like that. Coach Turner was like a drill sergeant; he didn't like nonsense. He didn't allow us to talk on the way to the game.

"Focus on the game!" he yelled. "If you win, then the ride home we can have some fun. If not, there's no celebration."

He held us to that. We lost the game by a touchdown, and he was pissed. The details of the loss are boring, and I don't feel like typing them all out. I found myself daydreaming during the game. After the game, he gave us a fiery speech, and then we had to be quiet the whole bus ride back to the school. I made a 23 yard field goal though. That was my excitement for the night. I still want to try a long one, but I don't think Coach Turner trusts me.

It sucks, because I told my parents I was going to go out with the guys after the game but the guys ended up not saying anything to me, so who knows if they went out. It was a somber, dark bus ride back, and nobody was in the mood to celebrate.

September 16, 1997

The football locker room is so much different than with soccer players. Soccer was tame; we just changed out of our uniforms and went home. These football guys made it a hangout in there. They liked to walk around half naked with their muscles glistening with sweat. I guess they felt like Roman soldiers who could take down whoever they wanted.

Todd Muler, our star wide receiver, who's this big, tall guy, I guess he is handsome. I can never tell with guys. I probably can, but I don't like to think of men that way. He looks like a big goof to me. Anyway, he was gloating about hooking up with Colleen Sanders, who's this really short girl, about half his size. He said they had sex and he "bottomed out" with her. I didn't understand what he meant. I knew it had something to do with sex, but I had never had sex, so it must have been some slang term. They all said he was bullshitting and then started laughing.

I don't understand why they like to hang out in the locker room. It smells awful. It must be a male bonding kind of thing. I was never a team guy or a bonding guy. I mostly stay on my own and don't work well with others. I guess that's why kicking is for me. I get to be on the team, but still do my job on my own, which works for me. It doesn't bother me that I'm looked down on as a lesser football player, or maybe not even a player at all. I'm just happy I have a uniform on and am doing something extraordinary.

Locker rooms remind me of prison. Well I've never been in a prison but from what I've seen in movies it is very similar. The communal showers filled with naked guys who are loudly talking and laughing, is a horrible sight. Some of the seniors look like fully grown men, even down there. I try not to look, but I get surprised sometimes, and I have to put my head down right away. I stay out of there as much as possible.

My routine is as soon as I get in the locker room after practice, I go to a dark corner and change real quick. I keep my back towards the wall because it is all red with acne. I hate my back. I'm on some medicine now that is supposed to help it. It seems to be working, but my face is all dried out, and I have to wear Chap Stick all the time. I have so many problems compared to the jocks. I think if I address these problems, one by one, I can be a better person in time. It just sucks, because once I fix one problem, another one pops up.

September 20, 1997

Another loss! This was a close one. We played South Chesterbrook, which I was told didn't have that great of a team. We were up most of the game, but then Jake threw an interception late in the game and they took it back for a touchdown, putting themselves up by three points. We never came back from that. We went four downs in a row and couldn't get the first down. They got the ball back with a minute left and ran out the clock.

Even though we lost, I have to admit that it kind of made me happy to see Jake mess up like that. For the longest time, it seemed like he was the type of guy who didn't make mistakes, but he is human like everyone else. He was so pissed in the locker room after the game. He was yelling and cursing and even punched a locker. The guys had to calm him down. I was nervous, because when guys like that get pissed, they can get violent and beat people up. I really don't know him well, but I didn't take any chances, I stayed out of his sight.

September 22, 1997

The teachers have been talking about taking the PSAT's again. They mentioned it a little bit last year but now they seem to be stressing it more. I have no desire to take them or the SAT's. I'm bad at both math and English. I like writing in my journal but I couldn't tell you the first thing about grammar. I don't even know if my sentences are complete. It's so stressful. Why should my decisions as a kid dictate the rest of my life? All I'm worried about is kicking and movies and music and cars right now. Nothing else interests me.

My guidance counselor asked me what I wanted to do and I told him I wanted to work as a mechanic or a movie reviewer. All he said was "ok" and then look at a piece of paper with my grades on it and said that if I wasn't taking the PSAT's, then I should sign up for a SAT prep course and take them in the spring time. It was like he was a robot with a certain set of instructions. Why isn't there something else other than the SAT's and college? I mean, I don't want to be working at Earl's for the rest of my life, but there should be some other path for kids who hate school.

September 25, 1997

I've never worked out in my life. It seems embarrassing to me. I don't want to be a football jock, but Jerry keeps harassing me. So today, I did it. I went into the weight room. It was everything I was expecting. Big goons grunting and lifting really heavy weights with 80's rock blaring in the background. They were so strong; I wanted to leave as soon as I got in there. I felt so small.

The room also had a strange smell, like a mixture between sweat and bleach. It made me want to throw up.

Jerry came up to me when I entered and started to show me how to lift free weights. Immediately, my body started to ache. I hated it. Then, he had me lie down on a bench and push up a bar with some heavy metal. I think I did 95 pounds.

"Man, you're skinny, but if you keep working out, you can be ripped!" Jerry said. "You have that type of body; you could have a six pack."

I was glad I knew Jerry. He was like my guardian angel. I hated lifting. I wanted to go home and watch TV. He was right; if I really worked out, I could have six pack. The problem is that I like eating cheese fries and Cocoa Puffs and burgers too much.

"Come on, one more!" he yelled.

Why do people do this, it's worse than running, I thought.

"Ok, I'm good," I said after a half hour.

"Good first day, well get you in shape soon enough."

Jerry said.

Little did he know I'm done. I want to be in shape and have muscles but it's too much work. Especially since I have to look at all the other guys, who are benching 300 pounds, so what was the point? I'm definitely not going back there.

September 26, 1997

Today in history class this girl Lola Millford was wearing a see-through shirt, and you could see her bra. Her cans were so big and wonderful. She is one of those white chicks who acts ghetto. Lola likes to wear thick makeup, and she makes her hair real shiny, like she just came out of the shower. I wonder what she puts in there to make it look like that. She hangs around with other girls that have the same look. They all smell like smoke and like to curse. I'm pretty sure any one of them could beat me up. I think Lola even dated a few black guys from public school. That was always intimidating, because they always seemed so cool, and I heard they had huge cocks.

I think she wishes she was black, when really she's an upper-middle-class white girl whose dad owns a chain of car dealerships. I see her roll into school in the morning with a new BMW, and she acts all boss. She could definitely pull off being black. But really, I would like to see her try and live in the real ghetto; she wouldn't last a day. She's all bad to the bone living in the white suburbs going to a Catholic school. Nerdy little white guys like me pose no threat to her. I have no image and I don't drive a cool car and I don't wear the right clothes. It's all a show in this place, and I have nothing to present.

September 27, 1997

We won our 4th game! It was at home against the Madison Bobcats, and we smoked them! I even made two field goals: a 22 yarder and a 27 yarder. Anything under 30 is automatic for me. It's when it gets over 30 that it can be hairy.

The game wasn't even the fun part. Jerry pretty much forced me into his car after the game and took me to a football party at Todd Muler's house. I asked Jerry if his parents were away or something, and he said "Nope, just wait." When we rang the doorbell, his mom answered!

It turns out that they're "cool parents." I had heard about cool parents before, but I didn't know it was a real thing. Cool parents were the type of people that knew their kids were going to drink and let them do it at home. They had a nice basement like Darcy's, and they let us drink beer down there. Nobody was allowed to drive home though; that was part of the rules.

I called my mom from Todd's house and told her I was sleeping over Ralph's. She said "no problem" and told me to "have fun." "Great game, you deserve it," she even said. I hate hearing praise from anybody. It is so embarrassing.

There were about 10 of us there playing pool and watching TV while we drank cheap canned beer. Todd's girlfriend, Collen, Katie Polk, and a few other football groupie girls were there as well. They were all really pretty, and I didn't have a chance with any of them. I stayed by Jerry's side most of the time and ended up getting kind of drunk. He got kind of annoyed after a while, and I saw him go into the bathroom with Katie for what seemed like a half hour.

I think I had five beers, which is a lot for me. I was starting to like drinking. Beer was starting to taste better, and the feeling is absolutely amazing. It seems like the more I drink, the less I care about what people think of me. I remember playing pool by myself at the end of the night. I used to do this when I was a kid and didn't have anybody else to play with. I ended up getting really good after a while. I guess I've always been like that. I really thrive in isolation, which is probably why I got so good at kicking. People are such a distraction.

I don't know what time I went to bed, but I remember Todd's mom coming down and giving everybody sleeping bags and pillows at some point. I saw Todd and Colleen go upstairs together. I asked Jerry about it the next day, and he said they always let Colleen sleep in Todd's bedroom. "That's insane!" I said. Jerry said Todd's dad used to play for Lindsburg so he thinks he's living through Todd now. My parents wouldn't let any of that happen in our house.

When I told Ralph about the party the next day, he couldn't believe it.

"It's like you're part of a secret society now."

"Yea, this was going on the whole time and Jerry never told us any of this."

He never did tell us what they were up to. It was strange, like he wanted to keep his two worlds apart. We were the backup "down to earth" guys he hung with, and the football guys were the more exciting option.

"It was fun, but I felt out of place," I said. "I didn't know what to say to them."

"Yea, it's not your world."

He was right; I was out of my element.

October 2, 1997

I have some really bad news. I got accused of cheating by Mr. Howard yesterday. He gave us a take home algebra test last week, and I did my usual routine:

get the answers, make up the work. Well, this time, he actually looked at my work. He wrote in big red letters on my test:

"THE WORK DOES NOT SUPPORT THE ANSWERS!! HOW DID YOU GET THE CORRECT ANSWERS? THIS SEEMS FISHY!"

Then, he wrote a big red zero on my test. I was shaking looking at the test. Part of me was relieved he just gave me a zero. He could have called the principal and told him that I had cheated. What am I going to do now? I know nothing about algebra.   I'm screwed!!

October 3, 1997

I was telling Darcy at lunch today what happened in algebra. She told me not to worry, "algebra isn't that hard." Then Cecilia said that she could help me out if I needed it.
"What do you need help with?" she asked.
"I don't even know. I don't remember anything from freshman year." I said.
"Oh geeesh. We're going to need a while."
"Yea, I hate numbers, never trusted them."
"Haha, why don't you bring your homework over to my house and well go over it."
"Ok, I got practice until six, so I can stop over after."
"Watch out Nic, this is how Cecilia lures all her

victims in. She promises good grades, and then they end up chained in her basement!" Darcy said trying to be funny.

"Shut up!" Cecilia said.

"Her family is weird, they're too clean cut, and I know they're up to something." Darcy said.

After practice, I drove over to Cecilia's house with my algebra homework. I really didn't feel like learning algebra after a long day. I was thinking if she could do my homework for me that would be awesome. Also, I could ask her about Darcy. Maybe she could tell her that I liked her, and then Darcy would know and *she* would ask *me* out. That's like a Jedi mind trick.

I showed up to her house that was down the street from Darcy. Her house wasn't as big but it was still impressive. I rang the bell and she answered the door. She was wearing a nice skirt and I could smell some perfume. Was she dressing up for me?

Cecilia let me through her big clean house while her mom cleaned up in the kitchen and her dad read the paper at the table. She introduced me, and they seemed like genuinely nice people. I didn't see anybody else there. I wondered if she had any siblings. She took me back to the dining room where it was quiet and we could study.

Sitting at the table with her, I realized this was the first time we were hanging out without Darcy. She was always the buffer between us. It felt awkward at first, so I brought up Darcy and said how crazy she was. She told me some stuff I hadn't heard, like that when

Darcy's brother got kicked, he started doing a

bunch more drugs and got some girl from North Park High pregnant.

"Wow, that crazy!" I said. "How old is the girl?"

"17. Yea, it's getting pretty crazy over there. YOU CAN'T TELL HER I TOLD YOU!" she stressed.

"Don't worry, I won't tell anybody. That is fucked up. Is Darcy dating anybody now?" I asked. "I can never keep track."

"Yea, some North Park guy she met at the mall. Guy is a total stoner, of course."

Fuck! When she told me that, it felt like someone came and slashed my tires. I was completely deflated and heartbroken. I think Cecilia knew I liked Darcy, because she then said "Don't worry, I don't think it will last. She gets bored quick."

"Oh, ok."

It did make me feel better.

I didn't know what to say so I asked about college. That was my standard question when I didn't know what else to say.

"I'm hoping to get into Penn State. My older sister's there now and she loves it," she said. "What about you?"

"I don't know. College scares me. I don't even know what I would do." I said truthfully.

"You'll figure it out. Hey, if this kicking thing keeps going, maybe you can get a scholarship."

"Haha, good one. I'm one bad kick away from being off the team. It's week to week. The pressure is intense."

When we finally got to the math, she was able to explain it in a way that I could understand. It might have been because I thought Mr. Howard is a dick, and I never pay attention. It turns out I'm not such an idiot. If I pay attention and actually try, I can learn something. I just hope I'll be able to retain it. That has been a problem of mine. Once the test is over, I forget everything.

We sat there for about two hours, and then I told her I had to leave.

"When is your next test?" she asked.

"Two weeks."

"Ok, good, we have some time to get as much math in that brain as possible. You need to practice every day, like football."

"Oh god," I said.

Driving home, I started to think about Darcy and this North Park guy. Yet again, screwed over, I thought. I'm forever in the friend zone. It should have happened by now. I need to evaluate my life.

October 4, 1997

I've been on the team for over two months now, and I still don't know much about the game of football. I know the quarterback hikes it and throws the ball to a receiver or hands it off to the running back, but not much else. I just stand on the sidelines and watch guys run all around; I don't even know the names of the positions. The only ones I know on defense are linebacker and defensive end because that's what Jerry and Ronnie are. The game kind of bores me.

We had our 5th game yesterday, and we lost again. I don't know what our problem is. It seems like our defense is on the field a lot. I think they're getting tired out and then the other teams take advantage.

At least I'm having so much fun kicking in front of all those people. I'm not even nervous anymore! Who would have thought? Not me, that's for sure.

More importantly, I rented this football movie that came out a few years ago called *Necessary Roughness*. The title is clever because in football there is a penalty called "Unnecessary Roughness" which is when a player hits someone after the play is dead. I only know that because Ronnie was running after a guy trying to tackle him, and the guy ran out of bounds and Ronnie hit him anyway. The ref gave him a 15 yard penalty.

Necessary Roughness is a comedy about an entire college football team in Texas that gets suspended from playing due to NCAA violations. They need to put a new team together, so the coach goes out and gets guys off the street with an open try out. The coach still needs a quarterback, so he finds a 30-something year old high school quarterback star who never went to college played by Scott Bakula, who starred in the show *Quantum Leap,* to join the team. He even gets a girl soccer player, a really hot Kathy Ireland, to be the kicker. Oh, and Sinbad plays a defensive player.

The movie is dumb, but I thought it was pretty funny. Not screw ball funny either. I hate that crap. Sometimes you need a dumb comedy to shut off your mind. I liked watching *Necessary Roughness* more than I liked watching real football. Mostly because the people in the film didn't take the game seriously like my teammates and the guys we were playing against.

The football jocks act like we're in the NFL and winning is life or death. I don't know; maybe it's me. It really doesn't matter to me; I see it as a dumb game. I only care about making my kicks. If I do that and we still lose, there isn't much I can do. Thank God. If I do miss a crucial kick, and we lose because of me, my ass will be toast. Luckily, that hasn't happened yet. I hope it never comes down to me having to win the game with a kick.

Necessary Roughness: 3/5 stars

October 7, 1997

My favorite teacher this year is Mr. Ulogard. He's my marketing teacher. He's a big guy, bald and has a huge belly. He likes to wear skin tight golf shirts for some reason. I think he must have gained a ton of weight and then didn't want to buy new shirts. I had no interest in marketing. I hated business. The only reason I took it was because it was a choice between either Spanish 3 or marketing, and I was done with Spanish.

Mr. Ulogard sits in front of the class on a stool and tells us these long stories about his life. He worked for a big company called Dupont as a sale executive in his youth and made a lot of money. He said he was a shark. I don't know what his actual job was, but it involved traveling around the country and going to meetings, making deals. He said he worked non-stop. No amount of money was making him happy. At 45, he had a massive heart attack and had to take a few months off work.

He saw it as his second chance at life and never went back. Instead, he went to school full time and got his teaching certificate. Now, he sits in front of a class of kids and tells weird stories about his life.

Yesterday, he told us about when he got married and didn't have sex with his wife until after they were married. He didn't even see her naked until their wedding night. He said when he saw her naked for the first time, he was expecting her vagina to look red, like red lipstick color. Everyone in the room looked around at each other and couldn't believe he was telling us this. It was so strange. It made sense, he got married in the 50's and a lot of people didn't have sex until they were married.

He's also notoriously cheap. He had some type of rebate system where he sent in expired coupons and then got sent a check for like 19 cents. I had never heard of this. He loved to haggle. He never paid full price for anything. He told us how to successfully beat a car dealer. I didn't even know you could low ball a new car, which kind of blew my mind.

We don't use the marketing text book that much. Around the end of the class, he looks at the clock and says "damn, we gotta do something for me to keep my job." Then he opens to a page and reads a few paragraphs and assigns homework.

Tests are a breeze because they're open book. Let

me clarify, IN CLASS tests are open book. We can use our books to find the answers. It is basically a like an in class assignment. I think this class is going to be my first grade A.

I love Mr. Ulogard more than Mr. Leyland. He gets it. High school is a waste of time, a holding period until we go to college. He's teaching us real world knowledge. Nobody in our class knows what is really out there. We've been raised in the white suburbs our whole lives. There isn't any crime around here. When I do hear of kids venturing into the city, it's like they're going to another country. They act so cool when they talk about the city because they walk around and see black people.

I see all these smarty pants honors students studying all day and showing off. Yea, they might get into a good college, but who cares? All that matters is getting into college. I know I'm not smart enough to get a scholarship, so I will just plod along and do just enough to get in. I like getting a real world education.

October 9, 1997

I picked up this really great CD the other day; it's called *Smash* by The Offspring. They're a fairly new rock band with a little punk in there. They have this one song on called *Self Esteem* and I can really relate to it. Why? It's about some loser guy who keeps getting shit on by a girl. That's me! These lyrics pretty much sum up the last year of my life:

Now I know I'm being used
That's okay because I like the abuse
I know she's playing with me
That's okay 'cause I've got no self-esteem

I think I've had enough of Darcy. I'm going to start looking for another girl to be obsessed with. It's weird, I have always been like that. I can only handle one girl at a time. My first crush was Carol Liefhoffer in 3rd grade, but she moved to North Carolina, and then I moved onto Laura Mitchell from 4th to 8th grade, then Darcy from 9th grade to now. I feel like I might be able to ask out one of the stoner girls since I'm on the football team now. I see them at the games, so that has be good for something.

Still, sitting across from Darcy every day, I know it's going to be hard to shake those feelings.

October 12, 1997

Wow, what a game! We played the Springfield Rams on Friday, and it was tied all the way until the end. We had the ball with 13 seconds left at the 26 yard line. Coach Turner called an end-zone pass, but Jake threw it over the receivers head, leaving four seconds left. I was warming up for a kick just in case. 43 yards was a long shot. I had made a 45 yarder in practice, but that was practice.

Coach Turner called a time out and the guys came over to the sidelines. Jake kept saying he wanted another shot at the end zone.

"I think we should give Walenti a shot at this. If he misses, we can still win in overtime," Coach Turner said.

I heard my name and ran over. "Everybody go line up for a kick!" he yelled.

Running out there, I was more nervous than I had ever been. At least it's tied, I thought to myself.

It was a cold October night, and the ball wasn't booming off my foot like back in September. I was going to have to really get a good hit on it.

"Hut, Hut, Hike!"

I got a nice clean hit, straight as an arrow. The ball glided through cold night air under the bright lights and went right on through the yellow uprights. I stopped breathing for about five seconds after, and then the whole team ran onto the field. 10 seconds later I was buried in sweaty football players. It was surreal.

I can't wait for school on Monday. I wonder if what I did in the game will transfer to school. I wish Darcy had been there to see it. She was probably doing drugs or something.

October 15, 1997

So my last minute heroism at the game seems to only be a hit with the teachers. They all congratulated me. Mr. Ulogard even pulled me aside after class and said I should start sending tapes to colleges. What the hell? That made me so nervous! I don't even want to think about that right now. Darcy just kind of gave me a snide remark at lunch. "Mr. Bigshot," she called me. I think she might be jealous. Of me. The skinny dork. What is going on? She must be used to me being a loser and she Ms. Popular, I can't think of anything else.

October 18, 1997

Another win for the Lindsburg Spartans! This season is flying by. We're starting to turn it around. Finally we are over .500. Our record right now is 4 and 3 (four wins, three losses). It's going to be hard to make the playoffs though, the best team is 6 and 1, and they're blowing everybody out.

Apparently, we lost a bunch of really good seniors to graduation last year so it's a rebuilding year for us. This is Jake's first year starting, so he's still trying to find his groove. This is all news to me because I never paid attention to football. The team was really good last year and almost won the state title. They were two games away. I think a lot has to do with Coach Turner. He's a really good coach; I'm surprised he isn't at a college coaching football.

October 19, 1997

Cecilia has been tutoring me for a few weeks now, and it's really sinking in. I can't believe it! I got my math test back and I got a B. I answered all the questions and showed my work like a real student. In the past I would just skip questions that I didn't know and just end up getting a barely passing grade. She was a really good teacher. Mr. Howard can suck a big one. It doesn't mean I like math now; I still hate every second of it. I'm so happy I don't have to cheat anymore. That never made me feel good. Not doing work is one thing. Cheating is kind of scummy.

I've been going over to Cecilia's house once a week, and it's like we're friends now. She told me some personal stuff that I wouldn't repeat to anybody, but I think it's ok to say it here since nobody will see it. Cecilia said she was a lot bigger when she was in grade school and got picked on all the time. She said Darcy tried to protect her as much as she could, but she couldn't be around all the time. I told her I understood and that I had a pretty brutal childhood as well.

She said that books became her retreat from the world. Cecilia showed me her bookshelf in her room, and it was enormous. She had read so many. I told her I hated reading, well, mostly. I told her that the few books that I had read were last summer were pretty good but I was more into movies. It was nice to hear someone else who wanted to escape the real world with fictional stories. Life is so much better when you're not trying to fit in all the time. I think it's perfectly acceptable to lose yourself in a good book or movie.

I asked her what was going on with Darcy.

"I don't know, she is stoned all the time now. She smokes on the ride to school every day. She doesn't seem to care about anything," she said.

"Wow, that sucks," I said.

Even at lunch, Cecilia and I are talking more and more. Darcy has definitely taken notice and told me not to steal her best friend. She can be so possessive sometimes. I don't even know who she's dating now, I can't keep track anymore. Sometimes, I hear she hooks up with a guy at a party and I never know if it is true or not. I find myself caring less and less. I know I'm becoming attracted to Cecilia; I just don't know what I'm going to do about it.

It's weird because she was there the whole time, but I just saw her as Darcy's fat friend. It's not even like she is that fat, it's just next to Darcy most girls don't look as good. I'm glad I'm getting to know her; maybe I'll ask her out if things keep going like they are. It's strange though. I never found her attractive before. That must be how girls get in your head. Like subliminal advertising. Not that I'm complaining, I'm ok with it!

It's so nice being in a good mood most of the time. I can't even tell you when the last time that I was happy on a day to day basis. I don't think I was ever.

October 25, 1997

We had the homecoming pep rally on Friday. It's never a good day for anybody but the popular kids. The losers always try to skip out. I remember freshman year they brought us into the gym and the whole school was already in there. They yelled at all the freshman to "go home" as we walked in and then they made us sit on the floor like dogs while everyone else was in the bleachers. I didn't understand what was going on. What was the point of it?

The rest of time, the football players and other upperclassman put on goofy skits. Even the teachers joined it. It was kind of funny, but I would have rather been at home, to be honest. I hated being in a large crowd like that, especially sitting on the floor for an hour. My butt started to hurt, and it was really uncomfortable.

At the end, the disciplinarian got on the mic and welcomed all freshmen to the school. He said we were formally accepted to Lindsburg Catholic. It was like hazing, we had to get beat up a little bit to become a part of something. It didn't make me feel any better.

On my bus ride home, I didn't feel anymore apart of the school. Nothing had changed for me. I sat alone on the bus, still ignored, still anxiously awaiting for my bus stop, so I could run home and forget about school.

This year, I was on the other side. It was so strange. Pep Rally days were always dress down days. All the football players were expected to wear their jerseys, so I put on my green Lindsburg jersey this morning and looked in the mirror. It was like I was different person. I looked really stupid in it without my pads. I'm too skinny for this, I thought. Football jerseys are for fat guys and muscular guys. I'm neither. I put on a backup shirt underneath just in case.

My mom loved it, she was so happy when I walked down the stairs. There was some hope in her eyes, like I'd never seen. It was too much pressure. I just wanted to go back to bed. That wasn't me. How does Jerry wake up and be a football player every day, like it's his calling?

So I walked into the hallways wearing my jersey. Ralph looked at me like I was an alien.

"Really?" he said.

"Ok, I'm going home," I said.

"Whatever man, just go with it, " he said.

I felt better when he said that. But I still felt like a sellout.

"Fuck it," I said, taking off the jersey and stuffing it in my locker. I had a Black Sabbath T-shirt on underneath it, which felt more like me.

I stood in the pep rally crowd and blended in with everybody else, which felt amazing. The really cool people like Jerry, put on skits like *Ghostbusters* and *Men in Black* and danced to M.C. Hammer wearing those goofy pants. A bunch of guys dressed up like the Village people and danced to the Y.M.C.A. song. I looked around and all the underclass girls stared at them like they were celebrities. They were larger than life. They could get any girl in the school. I wish I could be like that, I thought.

At the end, some of the really hot senior girls came out dressed up as Lindsburg football players and made fun of how macho they acted. That was pretty funny.

The homecoming game that night was against a really bad team, the Wannaque Knights. They didn't win a game all season.   In the first half, we smoked them 24-6.

At half time they presented what was called the "Homecoming Court."   This was five senior girls that were competing to be the Homecoming Queen. It was kind of like in those high school movies when at the end of the Senior Prom, they announce the Prom Queen. We didn't have that in our school; we had this instead. It was the first time I had seen this display in real life. I saw pictures in the year book in years prior but this was something else.

The girls came out with their dates and they walked on a red carpet out into the middle of the field, and then walked in a circle to wave to the crowd.   It reminded me of those dog shows on TV. I just sat on the bench and wondered when it would be over. The principal got on the mic and then announced the winner. I don't even know how they chose the winner. There might have been a vote, but I probably missed it. I didn't pay attention to those things. The girl who won was this super-hot thing who acted like she won the lottery. She jumped up and down and then hugged all the other contestants. The guy she was with looked happy too. He was definitely getting laid after the game.

The rest of the game was smooth sailing. We won the game 55-9. It wasn't even a contest. I believe they set up the homecoming game as an easy win for the home team. What if we lost? It would have been a somber day.

Blowout wins like that make my job easy. I only had to kick extra points and kick-offs, which is what I prefer. I had no desire to be a hero or a superstar.

October 26, 1997

I heard the best song today! It's called *The Lonesome Kicker* by Adam Sandler. I was flipping through the channels and the video was on MTV. Apparently Adam Sandler came out with a new comedy CD called *What's Your Name* and I didn't even know about it. I had listened to his last two albums over and over and still loved them. I was so excited that I went out to Circuit City right after I saw the video and bought the CD.

When I got home, I laid on my bed and listened to it straight through for an hour. Unfortunately, it wasn't that good. The skits were stupid, and the songs were just ok. It didn't even come close to *They're All Gonna Laugh at You* or *What the Hell Happened to Me*. The kicker song was really good though. I listened to it a bunch of times, and he really nailed what it's like to be a lonesome kicker. Here are the lyrics I copied off from the inside of the CD:

Me, I'm the Lonesome Kicker
Extra points, field goals at your service
One might think it comes with glory
You might think different after you listen to my story

My helmet is equipped with a tiny face mask
What it possibly could protect, I do not know

The other guys on the team
Like to make fun of my little shoulder pads
And also like to hide the special shoe
I need to kick in the snow

People think it's so easy
To kick a field goal from the 30 yard line
They forget to add seven yards for the snap
And 10 more 'cause the goal posts are pushed way back

In 1974, the uprights were right on the goal line
But some of the players were running into them
And getting hurt
So screw the kicker
Who cares about the kicker?

But I kick that ball
And I pray it goes straight
If it does
The coach says "Good job, number 8"
He doesn't even know my name is
Andre Kristacovitchlalinski, Jr.
But that's the life I live
The Lonesome Kicker

Kickoffs can be so very scary
Especially, if the returner breaks on through
And I'm the only guy on the playing field left to tackle him
I don't want to get hurt
So I pretend to tie my shoe

Once again, I'm ignored by my teammates and all my
coaches

183

"Go back where you came from!"
Scream 70,000 fans
Well, I know I could win their love back
By catching a winning touch-down
But, unfortunately, I was born with these very small hands

And I hope that the cameras don't come in too close
'Cause they might see the tears in my eyes
As I sit on this bench made of cold-hearted wood
And the splinters go deep in my thighs
And the towel boy snickers as he walks by
The Lonesome Kicker

Another blocked kick
And everybody blames me
But it was the Left Guard
Who didn't pick up his man
Oh, why can't they see...

In my home country
I could have been a minor league soccer player
But I came to America
Seeking fortune and seeking fame
I didn't realize that if I shanked one
And blew the point spread
Some drunk guys would push me into their hibachi
After the game

So I go home at night
'Cause I never get invited
To go drinking with the other guys
And I sit in my chair, and I soak my foot

As I eat a plate of cold french fries
And my wife's out with her quote-unquote friend
And my son can't look me in the eyes
But that's the life I live
The Lonesome Kicker

Kicking for you
They took my snow shoe
They're going for two

Really great lyrics, huh?! He really captures how the team doesn't give a crap about the kicker. Even though this album sucked, I hope keeps he making them, he's so funny.

November 1, 1997

So, I finally screwed it all up. It was bound to happen sooner or later, and this was a big one. I don't know if I want to be on the team anymore. I'll start near the end because really nothing else matters.

The score was 24-21 with 2 minutes and 4 seconds left on the clock. The Wellsville Cougars were beating us all game on their home turf, but our Spartans offense fought hard and got us to the 14 yard line. It was 4th and 2. Coach Turner would have normally gone for the touchdown because you never wanted to put the game in the hands of a high school kicker.

"Walenti, get over here!" Coach Turner yelled.

"Make this kick, and we'll hold them off, and take this into overtime. You got this!"

I just nodded my head and ran out to the middle of the field. I looked at the upright flags; still no wind. This was the most pressure I had all season but I was confident in my ability. If I had this kick early on, I would have been shitting my pants.

I took three steps back, two steps over, and was ready to knock in the tying score. I was already assuming we would win this game with my kick. I hadn't missed a big kick all season. I could already envision them carrying me off the field after the game.

"Hut, hut, hut, hike!" the backup quarterback Ryan Mikal yelled.

As soon as he said "hike," I started my motion. I looked up and the ball wasn't hiked on-time. It came out a second late, and I was already in motion to kick the ball. I had to stop a second and wait, then Ryan had the ball in position. I gave it a clumsy swing of the foot, and it sailed wide left. I stood and watched my high school dreams fly away. FUCK!

Everyone was stunned. My first big miss, I knew it had to come at some point. I looked over to the stands and saw my parents with looks of despair on their faces. My mother looked like she was ready to cry. I scanned the crowd and saw Darcy, she was standing next to her boyfriend and Cecilia, and when we made eye contact, Cecilia mouthed, "I'm sorry." I had let everyone down.

I looked away from the stands and walked back with my head down. The jeering of the Cougars fans surrounded me like stereo speakers in my helmet and made me want to run out of the stadium. They were all chanting, "Go back home, go back home, go back home!"

As I walked back to the sidelines, I could see that the team was deflated. I sold them a lie. Nobody wanted to hear that the snap was late and my timing was off. I had one job, make the kick. The team battled so hard to get me into decent range. A 31 yard kick should have been automatic. I was making 47 yarders in practice with no problem. I sat on the cold metal bench and put my head down in my hands. I was upset, and wanted to look dramatic and show everyone I felt like an idiot.

There were two minutes left. The Cougars offense took over on the 14. All they needed was one first down and the game was over. Of course, they ran the ball the first two downs getting seven yards. It was 3rd and 3, and they ran again and the defense stopped them a half yard from getting a first down! They let the clock run down and then punted. We got the ball at the 45 yard line with 34 seconds left. It was possible I would have to kick again. I got up and watched the quarterback throw two quick passes towards the sidelines. We were at the 24 yard line with 19 seconds.

I started warming up with my practice net. Was he going to put me in? Oh God, I hope not; I might puke, I thought. The quarterback heaved a beautiful spiral to the end zone and a cornerback from the Cougars jumped in front of the ball and intercepted it! The Cougar bench erupted, and the game was over. I let out a huge sigh of relief. I was off the hook.

Coach Turner was pacing along the sidelines and

was losing his mind. I had never seen him like that. He threw down his clipboard and walked out off the field and went right to the bus. The assistant coach stuck around and told everyone to get packed up. We needed to get out of there as fast as possible. The bus ride back was dark and quiet; nobody said a word. I knew they still wanted to beat my ass for missing that kick. When we got back in the parking lot, I grabbed my shit and didn't say anything to anybody. As I was loading my pads into truck, I got a tap on the back. I turned around, and it was Jake, the quarterback, and Willie the running back, towering over me. Here it comes, I thought - the pummeling I deserve.

"You get one warning, you fucking miss another kick like that, and you'd better watch your back," Jake said, as he pushed my shoulder against the car.

"Dude, it was a bad snap!" I said, trying to defend myself.

They didn't care, they just walked away looking pissed off. I watched them and the other players gather around a luxury SUV with some cheerleaders. They were going out drinking, as usual, but this time, I wasn't invited.

It was then I realized that I wasn't part of the team. If I had made that kick then, it would be party time for me, but I didn't, so they turned their backs on me. It was a week-to-week season for the place kicker. If you didn't put your body on the line for the team, you were a mercenary, a specialty player. It didn't matter that I wore the same jersey as them or that I could win the game with a swift kick of my foot; they would never accept me.

I started my El Camino and drove home. When I walked in the door, I smelled a fresh pizza and my mother ran towards me.

"I'm not hungry, just going to bed," I said to her at the doorway. She came up and put her arms around me anyway. I kept my arms at my sides and felt like a kid again. It was like when I would have a bad soccer game in youth sports and my mom would try and comfort me and tell me that I was special. It was bullshit. I didn't want that anymore.

I could hear noise in the background and assumed my father was sitting in the den, watching TV as he usually was. I was glad he didn't try to cheer me up. I know he was disappointed and was never the type of man to give me words of encouragement. I slowly trudged, up the stairs and my mother yelled, "Just remember it's only a game!"

Just a game? What does she know? This is my life. It all rides on my foot. College, friends, popularity, it's all in my stupid foot now. How did I get myself into this? A few weeks ago, I was at a real high school party and was on my way to becoming somewhat popular.

Now, I was lying on my bed, alone, almost in tears. I couldn't take it. I reached under the bed and grabbed a bottle of mint schnapps I had stolen from Ralph's house. His dad had countless bottles of liquor that he didn't keep track of. I took a long pull straight from the bottle, and my mouth immediately tasted like a candy cane. It felt good. I took another swig, put my headphones on and pressed play on my Discman. Nirvana blared through my head all night long until I passed out.

My mother let me sleep until noon today, and I just stayed in the house all day and watched TV. Ralph called me to see how I was doing, but I told my mom to tell him I wasn't home. I didn't want to see or talk to anybody. Hiding was my default setting when it came to things like this. I didn't do well confronting my problems. Sitting here at 9:00 in my room alone on a Saturday night is really depressing, I think I'm going back to bed now.

November 3, 1997

I woke up on Sunday morning with a different attitude. I was ready to shut everyone up. I grabbed my footballs and tee and went back to where it all started: the abandoned baseball field. That's where I kicked best. Out there by myself for a good year with just the rabbits, bugs, and the occasional groundhog, I really learned to concentrate and work on my craft. It was the only thing that calmed me down. Out there in the field, I kicked balls over the aluminum fence backstop for a good three hours. I hit every one of them. I even drilled a 60 yarder barely over the cage. My confidence was back!

At school on Monday, I wasn't sure what to expect from the team. They all crowded around their lockers in their varsity jackets before class started. I walked by, and they all shunned me. Then, out of nowhere, a big cornerback whacked my books out of my hands. They all started laughing as I picked them up and basically ran away. As I got down hall, I looked back, and they were still all laughing. I assumed it was at me, but I couldn't be sure. Oh well, back to the old Nic, I thought.

At lunch, I sat down, and I could see the sadness in Cecilia's eyes. Darcy didn't seem bothered and spoke first.

"So what the hell happened out there? I thought you never missed?" she asked.

"Nic shit his pants, that's what happened!" Gary chimed in.

"Yea, looks like my kicking days are over. I'll be surprised if coach doesn't give me boot. It's back to being a loser," I said.

"Now you're being rational, haha," Ralph laughed. "You don't go from being an anonymous nobody to a football hero. This ain't the movies."

"Stop it you guys, it was just one game," Cecilia said.

"I don't know. It would be really easy to quit and go back to my easy, boring life. Nobody expected anything, and it was amazing. Being hidden in plain view is underrated," I said.

"Stop, I think it's pretty cool you came this far," Cecilia said.

Ah, delightful Cecilia, always on my side.

"Well, you gave it a good shot. Maybe you can be the mascot next year," Darcy said.

Darcy was really loving this. She was reveling in my fall from grace. I was happy she was dating some scumbag date-rapist guy. I used to think she was too good for that, but not anymore. She deserves everything she gets.

As I ate, I glanced at the table in front of me to see Jack Cleasock, putting his foot up Lisa Morrisey's dress! It was the craziest thing I ever seen. He removed his one shoe and was sticking his foot right up there; what balls, I thought. And by the look on her face, she was into it! It doesn't surprise me; guys like that do whatever the hell they want, and chicks love that. Still, I couldn't believe what I was seeing. I looked around and nobody else seemed to notice. It went on for another for 10 minutes, and I didn't say anything to anybody. The bell rang, and I snapped back into reality.

It was weird that I saw that. Mostly because I was the only one. It was like a private thing between two people and wasn't meant for my eyes. I wonder if Jack broke up with Jaime or he's just a dog and cheats on her. Probably the latter; it seems that all these drug and jock guys don't give a shit about women. The girls must be cheating too. I really don't know. Why didn't I just do drugs and smoke cigarettes to get girls? It would be so much easier than what I was doing.

I'm thinking about quitting the team. Again, I don't even really like football! The whole field goal kicking was just a stupid scheme I came up with to get Darcy's attention, and that didn't even work. She's never going to want to date me.

Now shit is getting real. Kicking on the baseball field all alone was one thing, but another missed kick, and I'll be hung out to dry, and I'll earn a possible beating by Jake. The coach couldn't chance it either. They still had the old kicker Brad who is decent enough.

If I didn't pull my weight, they would cut me and use him.

November 5, 1997

I went over to Cecilia's tonight. I didn't even need any help with math; I just wanted somebody to talk to, although I told her I needed some help with my homework. Cecilia started out by showing me what inverse elements were, and then, when she saw me zoning out, she asked me if I was ok. I told her that I wanted to quit the team, and she said that was the dumbest thing she had ever heard.

"Huh?" I said.

"Fuck that, you're a really good kicker. It wasn't even your fault that you missed it," she said.

"I know, but all week the whole team has been ignoring me."

"You need some confidence. Shit, just give it another game and see what happens."

"Yea. Thanks."

It's funny, that was the first time I heard Cecilia curse and it was kind of hot. If anyone else would have told me that, I wouldn't have believed them. But I trust her for some reason. Sitting in her room - yes, we go in her room now, with the door closed - staring into her pretty blue eyes, I felt myself falling for her. I wanted to kiss her so bad but I couldn't. I was so scared. What do you do? I've seen so many movies in which the guy leans in, and the girl says "What the hell do you think you are doing?"

Instead, we went back to Algebra for a bit and then I told her I had to leave. She gave me a big hug at the door and I felt my whole body relax.

When I left, I was feeling so much better. She was right; I was a pretty damn good kicker. I worked so hard and to give it all up for one mistake would be insane. Still, Jake is pretty scary.

November 8, 1997

Phew! Things are sort of back to normal. Even though we lost last night's game, I did what I had to do. I made three field goals, 18, 23, 32 yards, made all my extra points, and had a really long kickoff that landed behind the end zone of the other team! I really didn't get many congratulations though. The team was too pissed off that they lost. I was simply ignored which is fine with me. I avoided an ass beating for at least a week.

November 15, 1997

The last game of the regular season, and we won again! Our final record was 6 and 5 and it wasn't enough to get us in the playoffs. I'm secretly happy because I just wanted the season over with. I miss going home after school. It's going to be awesome to have so much more time to watch movies and I can go back to working at Earl's again. I've been so broke lately.

We only have one more game left and that's the Thanksgiving Day game against our rivals, the North Park Owls. They've beaten us 13 straight years, which seems crazy. It kind of makes sense though, they have over 2000 kids at their school, and we have 600. Mathematically, that gives them a much better chance at getting better players.

November 18, 1997

I went over to Cecilia's on Monday for our usual math session. We were sitting there trying to go over some problems for the test on Thursday. I don't even know what it was, I was just anxious and couldn't pay attention.

"Do you want to go grab some food?" I asked her.

"Haha, I could tell you didn't want to study. Where?"

"Let's go to the diner. I can drive."

"Yea, I could go for some junk food."

She got in my car, and a look came upon her face. It was a confused look, like she didn't know what kind of machine she just stepped into. I started the car and she goes "Wow, that's really loud." I didn't know if that was a compliment or a jab. I put on *Slow Ride* by Foghat on the CD player, and we were off.

When we got to the diner, we ordered some cheese fries and two cokes. We sat and talked about how much we hated Lindsburg, and how all the kids were assholes, and how crazy Mr. Ulogard is. I told her I finally decided that I wanted to take my SAT's but was still scared.

"That's great! You really should try to get into college, I think you could do well if you study," she said.

"I know, it's so hard to concentrate. I wish I was like you. It seems like you can pick stuff up right away. I just tune everything out."

"It's a skill, like football. If you do it more, you'll get better," she said.

"What the hell are we going to do when we graduate? Seriously, do you even know what you'll major in?"

"Honestly, I don't know either. I think I 'll figure it out when I get into college."

It felt good to know that an honor student like Cecilia was as lost as I was. She had the grades though, I was jealous of that. Math was now my best class because of her. The rest of my classes were still C's. I felt like such a dummy when I was around her. All I can do is play video games and kick a stupid ball. I wish I was book smart like her; life would be so much easier.

"So, are you ready for the big Thanksgiving Day game?" she asked.

"Yea, ready for it to be over!" I said sarcastically.

"Haha, I haven't been to one yet."

"Me neither. Are you going to go?" I asked.

"Maybe. I never feel like myself at those games. I only go if Darcy goes, and I know she won't be up that early in the morning."

"Yea, I completely understand, I hated sitting in the stands. I barely watch the game from the sidelines, even nowadays."

"Haha, that's funny. Tell you what, if you can get an A on the next math test, then I will go."

"Come on!"

"That's the deal. Take it or leave it," she said.

"Ok, I don't have much of a choice here. I just wish we had studied tonight."

"You can come over tomorrow."

November 20, 1997

I took the algebra test today, and I could have gotten a C or an A, I really don't know. Some of the questions I know I got, others are a maybe, and a few, I definitely didn't answer right. So what does that mean? God, I hope Mr. Howard grades on a curve. He's been doing that the last couple of tests. I really want to win that bet with Cecilia even though nothing happens if I lose.

I asked Mr. Howard when we'll get the tests back, and he said "Probably Monday, depends on the weekend." I don't know what that meant. Maybe he drinks every weekend or something. Wouldn't surprise me.

November 22, 1997

It was so nice not to have a game on Friday. They gave us a week off before the Thanksgiving Day game. I just stayed in and rented a movie. It wasn't much of a decision, since Howard's Stern's movie *Private Parts* just came out on VHS. I wanted to see it in the theater, but it came out before I got my license, so it never happened. I've been listening to Howard almost every day since the summer and I know the whole cast of his show now.

The movie turned out to be one of my favorites. It went back to when he was a kid and showed how he became the number one DJ in the country. It's an amazing story because he was a bigger nerd as a kid than I'm. He just kept at it though; nothing stopped him from being the best.

The program director was this slim ball he called pig vomit because he looked like a pig and it made Howard want to vomit. He was Howard's arch nemesis, hired by the radio bosses to try to get Howard fired. Even with pig vomit trying to get him fired, Howard persevered, and eventually his ratings climbed to the top. The radio suits were baffled. They had no other choice but to fire pig vomit and give Howard whatever he wanted. The ending was so uplifting. It was like David and Goliath.

Tonight, I went over Ralph's house, and we ended up hanging with Chuck in his grand mom's basement. We drove around, and got really high, and didn't do much, and then went back and watched TV. Chuck went over to Romano's and got us free chicken fingers and wings, which was awesome. He was so lucky that he got all that free food.

I don't even like smoking pot. It makes me feel so stupid. I just do it when other people are smoking. It does relax me, but I hate driving home when I'm stoned. I get so paranoid. And then I get scared that I'm driving too slow or fast. I can never tell, because my El Camino's speedometer is broken. Getting high does make writing easier, I will tell you that. I'm sitting here at 2:00 in the morning and my mind feels so open. I can talk about anything right now.

Like the time in fourth grade that I was pretending to stab myself in class, and my teacher, Miss Leminor asked me what I was doing.

"I'm trying to kill myself," I said in front of the class.

She grabbed my arm and took me out of class.

"Why are you doing that?" she asked.

"I don't know. I'm joking, I guess."

"Ok, good."

Then we went back in class like nothing happened. I knew what I was doing; I really didn't want to kill myself, but I was thinking how easy it would be to be dead. By 4th grade, I was just so sick of it all: the kids, the homework, the tests, the playground, the whole mess of life. I had to lie to the teacher. If she called my mom, it would be a mess of therapists and counselors. Even at that age, I knew better. Maybe I was just crying out for attention. I only remember school as being a hell taht I couldn't escape. Ok, I'm going to bed.

Oh yea,

Private Parts: 5/5 stars

November 24, 1997

I got my test back today and I got an A-! It was my first A in math, ever. And it's probably going to be my last. I don't care though; this was the one that counted. When I got out of class I proudly showed my grade to Cecilia and she gave me a big hug. It was pretty cool. I told her it was really her grade because I'm a pretty dumb guy. She said I was too hard on myself and then we walked to lunch together.

November 27, 1997

Here we are again, Thanksgiving Day, one year later. I can't believe how much has happened since I started this journal. Looking back, I'm kind of proud of myself. I got through some really hard times. Still no physical contact with a girl, which kind of sucks - dancing with Sabrina Walder at the sophomore prom doesn't count.

I'm sitting here, at 6:00 am writing this before the last game of the season. We have to be at the North Park cafeteria at 8:00am for a breakfast with the other team. It's a tradition that every year the Lindsburg Catholic team and the North Park team meet before the Thanksgiving Day game to have breakfast together.

I'm more anxious about the breakfast than I'm the game. I hate having to eat with people, I don't know. I'm so bad at coming up with small talk. Forcing conversation should be illegal. Seriously what's the point? They don't care what I have to say, and I don't care what they have to say. Hopefully, I can get a seat next to Jerry or Ronnie, and then I'll just listen to them and then laugh like I'm having a good time. Ok, I better get a shower and get ready...

November 28, 1997

We did it. We fucking did it!!!! North Park's streak of 13 Thanksgiving Day wins has come to an end. I can't believe we won! It was the most exciting game of the season.

First, a summary of the breakfast. It was weird, and the North Park goons are worse than our guys. A lot of them were straight up dumb. They were big block heads that looked like the light upstairs was dim. I had to sit at a table with a bunch of 3rd stringers for both teams. All the starters sat together at a table and talked about football. Nobody at our table wanted to talk about football, so I started asking them about video games and movies. They were actually pretty cool guys. Not actually cool; they were kind of geeky and scrawny like me, but they liked a bunch of the same movies as I did.

In the locker room before the game, the guys were going nuts. They were yelling and trying to get all pumped like I had never seen. They wanted this game so bad. I sat on the metal bench in there and watched them act like apes. It looked ridiculous, but I wasn't a real football player, so I assume that's what they need to do to get pumped up. Before the other games, they weren't acting psychotic like that. This was a special game.

Coach Turner came into the locker and yelled for everyone to be quiet. As always, he gave us a motivational speech. This time, it was about how we had made it through a hard fought season and this was our last chance to show these public school punks how to play football. He said it was his privilege to coach such a good team, even though we didn't make the playoffs. Then Father Thompson came in and said his last prayer of the season.

I never said anything about it all season, but I hated the prayer. Why did we need to pray to God to help us win? It seems like we would be bothering God with some ridiculous prayer about a stupid high school football game. If there is a God out there, he should only be bothered with real issues, like murder and stuff.

At the end of the prayer, we all put our hands in the middle, and then we yelled "Go Spartans!"

When we got out to the field, the stands were packed, and I mean *packed* to the brim. I looked around and it was mostly parents. It was weird too, because it was 11:00 in the morning. All of our games prior were at night, which made it a fun night out for the high school kids. A lot of them had Thanksgiving Day plans so they couldn't make it. Darcy was nowhere to be found, so was Ralph and Greg and Bill. Bunch of bums. The luster of me being on the team had worn off.

In the middle of the stands, I saw Cecilia by herself. I waved and smiled. She waved back with her cute mittens. She kept her promise; nobody ever has been so nice. Of course, my parents were there and I reluctantly waved. My mom was taking a zillion pictures.

It was cold that morning but it was warming up as the sun came out. The frost was melting at a rapid pace, and the grass was going to be slick. Not good for anybody.

The North Park team won the coin toss and decided to receive the kick off. From there, things got worse. North Park dominated us from both sides of the ball. They racked up 24 straight points, it was looking like a route. We were able to get in field goal range, and I banged through a solid 35 yarder, and then we got a fluke long bomb touchdown to Todd Muler near the end of the half to keep us in the game. The locker room was ugly though.

Coach Turner gave us a half time brow beating like I had never seen. He laid into us that we were a bunch of pansies that didn't deserve to wear the uniform, and said if we plan to play like we did in the first half, we might as well go home now. He was really hot. Then Jerry, Willie, Jake, and Todd got up and started yelling to get everyone back into the game. "This is our last chance; we gotta punch these fuckers right in the mouth!" Jake said. Everybody screamed, even me. He is a charismatic motherfucker, I thought. No wonder he gets so many girls.

Also, at half time, they brought out all the old guys, and had a short alumni game. I didn't get to see most of the game, since we were being scolded in the locker room, but I did catch the last five minutes. Some of the guys were really old, like in their 50's! It was surprising that even the younger guys were all fat. All of them. Some were bald too. They were in their 30's, I think, and they looked like hell. I hoped I don't look like that someday. I would rather be fat than bald though. Definitely.

In the second half, we came out like a tornado. We got the kick off, and our returner took it to their 35 yard line. It sparked a wave of momentum right off the bat. The guys went out pumped up, and Willie, the running back, ran it all the way to the 5 yard line. Then, they gave it to him, and again and he was right in for a touchdown. All the sudden, it was a game again.

The next few possessions went back and forth; our defense was fired up and wasn't letting them get anywhere. Our offense cooled off a bit too. There were a few dropped passes, and Willie fumbled it in the red zone (inside the 20 yard line) and gave it back to North Park, which made Coach Turner rabid.
In the 4th quarter, with eight minutes left and the score still 24-17, our offense was at North Park 30 yard line.

It was forth down. I had been warming up for a few minutes and was ready to go for a field goal if we needed it. Coach called me over and asked "We need some points here, Walenti. It's 47 yards, what do you think?"

I looked at him dumbfounded. He never asked me anything before; it was like he was talking to me like an adult. I didn't want to answer, I was so scared. He smacked me on the helmet "Hey, kid!" he yelled.

"Oh, yea, gimme a shot," I said without thinking. What was I supposed to say? Thinking about it now, he wouldn't have asked me if he didn't think I could do it.

"I thought so, I've been watching you in practice, you definitely got the distance. Get out there."

It was the longest conversation with Coach Turner I ever had. Running out there, I kept my head down and didn't look at anybody or anything except the yellow uprights. I was glad it was daytime because there were no lights to deal with.

We lined up, the ball was hiked, and I gave it a worthy boot. For the first time, I turned away from the ball because I didn't want to watch it. I was too afraid of that image of the ball missing would be burned in my brain forever. It would be the end of my kicking forever. All I heard was raucous cheering and then a lineman picked me up from behind and gave me a bear hug.

Looking back, I wish I had watched it, because I want to know how close it was. Oh well.

The ball went back and forth a few times with no scoring; our defense really stepped it up and kept us in the game. I wasn't paying much attention but I heard one of the guys say that since we started "blitzing" in the second half, we were doing so much better. I don't know what that means. I'll have to ask my dad at some point.

Anyway, my fingers are getting tired and I'm getting bored talking about football. I need to wrap this up.

Fast forward, the game came down to the last 30 seconds. We had the ball on the North Park 12 yard line with the score still at 24-20. Since we kept getting stopped in the red zone, the coach called this really gutsy play where the quarterback handed it off to the running back and then the quarterback ran down as a receiver. It totally confused North Park. So Jake was wide open in the end-zone, and Willie threw a perfect pass to him, and we won the game! I didn't even know that was a legal play.

The stands were going nuts. It was a like a scene out of a movie. I couldn't believe I was there.

As the team celebrated in the locker room, doing god knows what, I got some pictures with my parents, and then met up with Cecilia after the game. We sat in her car in the North Park parking lot for about a half hour and talked. I don't even remember what we talked about but it seemed like five minutes.

She is such a nice and caring person. I wanted to kiss her so bad, but I was too much of a wimp. She even grabbed my hand at one point and gave me that face like she wanted a kiss but I still couldn't do it. AHHHH! I'm such a pussy! I just hugged her like a friend outside my car, and she left to go to her Thanksgiving meal at her grandparents. I met up with the rest of the team, and we took the bus back to Lindsburg.

December 5, 1997

It's been a week since the Thanksgiving game, and life seems to be going back to normal. It's a different kind of normal now. I walk the hallways with my head up, and I see people smile at me like I'm an actual person. I'm still the same old Nic but I don't care what people think anymore. Well, of course I care...being liked in high school is pretty much the most important thing there is right now. It's just easier to brush off people who are assholes and try to be around the ones that aren't. It's hard though, because most of the assholes are really cool and popular.

I don't think I'll ever get over my introversion and shyness. I have to learn to live with it and use it to my advantage. It's the only way I'm going to get ahead in this life. Even if I become a really good kicker someday, I'll never be like Jerry. He was born that way and will always be a social person. I'm going to have to work harder to get what I want, that's all I know.

So, I decided I was going to ask Cecilia to the Winter Dance. I had to; I couldn't stop thinking about her. Instead of asking Cecilia to the dance in person, which I could have easily done, I left a note in her locker, like I had wanted to do with Darcy. Here's what I wrote:

Dear Cecilia,

*I want to thank you so much for tutoring me these last
few months. You are such a good teacher! I'm still learning,
so I might need some help next semester. Right now, my grade
is a B, which is the highest it's ever been.*

*It has also been amazing getting to know you. I never
had a girl who was a friend before. You were always "Darcy's
friend," but now I see you as Cecilia, a really cool girl who's
super smart and funny.*

*I'm really bad at asking people to dances, but would
you want to go with me to the Winter Dance? I know;, it's so
cowardly to write a letter but I feel more comfortable with this
than actually asking. I think you'll be the one person who
would understand! It's something I need to work on.*

Nic

I put it in her locker after lunch and wasn't even
nervous about it. I was 100% certain she would say yes
or I wouldn't have asked. That's how I operate; I never
take big chances with girls like that. It is too risky.

At the end of the day, I opened my locker, and
saw a note stuffed in the vent. I opened it, and it said:

Hi Nic,

*I would love to go with you to the dance! Thank you
for the nice words, I was happy to give you a hand with
algebra. If you ever need any help, let me know!*

Cecilia

I looked at the letter, and something came over my whole body - happiness. A different kind though. It was so much better than when I made the football team. This was acceptance as a person from a another human being who is a girl. Or maybe the anticipation of some kind of romance. Really, I don't know? I never experienced those feelings before. It has always been longing, which is only one-sided.

Any other girl would think it was weird I wrote them a letter but not Cecilia. She was totally cool with it. It felt so strange to have a real date to a dance, not some girl who went with me out of pity.

Suddenly, nobody else mattered anymore. The bullies, the stoners, the jocks…it was all meaningless. I thought about how I worked so hard to get some attention and be some popular guy. I was exhausted. I just wanted to be myself again, the charade was over.

I closed my locker and walked down the hall towards Cecilia's locker. I could see her down the hallway on her tip toes trying to find something in the top part of her locker. As I walked, the rest of the people in the hallway were a blur. I didn't' even see them; it was like they didn't exist. I walked up to Cecilia like never before. Things were different now.

"Hey," I said.

"Hi."

We both looked at each other and smiled. Neither one of us knew what to say next.

Made in the USA
Middletown, DE
15 April 2017